The Time Curse

A Paths of Doom™ Adventure Book

by James M. Ward

margaret weis
productions, ltd.

PATHS OF DOOM is a trademark of Margaret Weis Productions, Ltd.

This book is dedicated to my mother and father who are very much missed in my household. I trust they are happy wherever they've gone.

THE TIME CURSE

Cover and interior art by Alberto dal Lago.
First Printing: January 2007
Printed in the U.S.A.
10 9 8 7 6 5 4 3 2 1

ISBN-10: 1-931567-72-7
ISBN-13: 978-1-931567-72-5

Margaret Weis Productions, Ltd.
253 Center St #126
Lake Geneva, WI 53147
Tel 262-725-3518
Fax 262-725-3521

Visit our websites:
www.pathsofdoom.com
www.margaretweis.com

You've picked up an exciting story that you read a bit differently than normal books. In reading a Paths of Doom book, you quickly begin to enjoy the characters and the action. During the first important action of the story, you—the reader—are offered a choice. It's your decision what the main character does next!

The process reads something like this:

The hero wants to go bravely forth and attack the enemy. *Go to page 999.*

The hero decides to be more careful and check for traps. *Turn to page 888.*

You make the choice, turn to the proper page, and continue reading—but the story's main character is acting the way you decide. Each time you make the important choices for the character and go to the suggested page to continue the story. It's up to you if the exciting adventure comes to a successful ending or the main character faces a terrible doom!

When reading a PATHS OF DOOM book, you can go back and experience the adventure again, following a new and different path each time.

Enjoy!

Seventeen year old Bren headed for home, making his way through the familiar crowded streets of Dragon City, whistling cheerfully as he went. Today's sword and dagger practice had been terrific, with him not making one mistake—for the first time—and he'd finally managed to keep Sword Master Trign from disarming him even once. In fact, Trign had said Bren could likely hold his own now in real combat.

Not that a merchant's son was likely to see combat. Still, Bren told himself, anything was possible.

The front door to their house was half-open. Well, that wasn't unusual when his merchant father was seeing customers. Bren thought his father wouldn't appreciate a shouted a greeting. Instead, the boy headed towards their main room just to see what was happening—then stopped short as he realized he'd arrived in the middle of a noisy argument.

Tawilden, his father, was not the one making all the noise. He was trying to talk calmly to three shouting priests—or at least Bren assumed from their flowing red robes that they were priests. They wore black leather armor over the robes. Each of the angry three had a wolf's head emblazoned in gold on his armor—and each of them was calling on their wolf god for help in dealing with this "stubborn barbarian." Tawilden was standing between them and his Tomtek jar collection, as though guarding it.

Bren was already man-tall and cat-quick. Hand on his dagger's hilt, he moved closer to see if he was needed. But his father calmly waved him away.

"It's just another group wanting to buy my Tomtek jars, son. You go on. I'll keep telling these priests no until they believe me."

The Tomtek jars were four hand-spans tall and made of milk-white alabaster stone. Each jar had a different head—always of some fabled creature—for a lid. Tomtek jars were commonly used in temples to hold holy lotions or spices. Some were said to hold souls — even those of deities.

Bren never could understand his father's love of collecting the jars, which the man had been doing since before Bren had been born. Occasionally, someone would come here trying to buy a jar or two. Tawilden, a master merchant who could likely sell fresh water to thirsty sharks, loved the jars far too much to part with any of them.

It really did look as though his father could easily handle the situation. The boy headed off for a quick wash-up and grabbed some dinner from the kitchen. But then

Bren hesitated. Swordplay and pretending he was a wild adventurer was a lot of fun. He was already his father's business partner. Like it or not, he had promised to get some accounting work done before he went to bed.

An hour of numbers later, the priests finally left with wolf howls of irritation and threats of curses on Tawilden and the rest of the house. Tawilden walked into the study where Bren was still going over accounts.

"So much for that lot," the man said with a grin. "They're not likely to bother us again. Hey, now, Bren, it's late. Go to bed, son. You need your sleep. You know the Merchant's Adage."

Bren could have recited it in his sleep. "Tomorrow is another day, with gold pieces to be earned along the way."

He gave his father a quick hug and went to bed. The swordplay had tired him out, as had that eye-tiring and not as much fun accounting work. Bren was asleep almost at once.

The next morning, feeling nicely rested, Bren sniffed the air as he got out of bed, expecting to smell breakfast. His father was an early riser, no matter what time he had gotten to bed the night before. However, Bren didn't smell a thing.

That's strange, he thought.

Of course, it was always possible that this one time his father had actually overslept. Just the same, Bren quickly dressed, armed himself with his favorite sword and dagger, and hurried downstairs to the main floor.

He stopped short in horror. "Father!"

The man was lying on the floor in front of the now-empty shelves that had held his collection. Bren raced to his side. His father had been badly beaten, but thank all the gods, he was still alive. He was unconscious and didn't open his eyes, no matter what Bren did.

Terrified, Bren called for the local healer-priest, an old man who worked both with medicine and magic, and had known the family since the boy's birth. "Bren, something is very wrong."

"But the injuries—they don't look bad."

"They aren't, not the visible ones. Those I can heal. But I sense some type of evil pressing deeply on Tawilden's mind."

"There were wolf priests here yesterday—they cursed him! No, both of us!"

The healer was staring at the shelves that had held the Tomtek jars. "I sense anger swirling about these empty shelves. It's so strong I could almost swear some furious deity—or something darker—was in the room."

"But what can I do?" Bren asked. "How can I help my father?"

"One jar," the healer said, his voice strange, as if he had slid into a mystic trance. "You must find the one jar."

"One! But they were all stolen!"

"You will know this one, not from its lid, but from the glyph carved into its base." In the next second, the trance was broken. In a more normal voice, the healer continued, "Bren, this will be no easy task. But you must return that jar to its shelf, then call in whatever priests you most trust. What I've done to heal your father will keep him from death for two weeks at most. If the jar isn't returned by then … your father will die."

"I'll find that jar!" Bren swore. "I will save my father's life!"

Bren thought the best thing to do would be to stay at home, so he could keep an eye on business, and to send hired men out to hunt for the jar. *Turn to page 18.*

Wren decided he'd better be the one to search for the jar. *Turn to page 36.*

Thanks to the gnome, Bren instantly appeared in his father's bedroom. His father lay motionless, breathing faintly but steadily—but over him stood two strangers in blue priestly robes who were glaring down at him in frustration. The priests carried staffs carved to look like serpents—of course, Bren thought, these had to be two snake priests. Not all snake priests were evil, just as some snakes were beneficial, but this wasn't the time or the place to figure out who they were. Bren hastily drew his sword.

"What are you doing in our home?" he cried.

The two priests turned sharply to him. "We were tricked," one of the men hissed. Both of them took out two snake-head lidded Tomtek jars from their packs. "We were sold these jars by the wolf priests, who swore your father told them the jars belonged to the Snake God. But these are not those jars! We want the correct jars."

"The wolf priests were the liars," Bren retorted. "Go curse them! They stole my father's jars and cursed us."

The two priests took a step back at that and raised their snake staves protectively in front of themselves.

"If I don't get the right jar returned soon," Bren explained tensely. "My father is going to die. Those jars you have are staying right here."

One priest aimed the tip of his staff at Bren. The second held his hand. "The lad is right, and these jars do us no good. Besides, can't you see the dark magics surrounding both their bodies?"

Startled, Bren glanced at his father and then himself, but could see no darkness around either of them.

"If we kill them," the second snake priest continued, "the curse will transfer to us. Leave the jars. We must strike at the lying thieves of wolf priests."

He waved his staff in a circle, hissing a spell, and the two of them vanished.

When they were gone, Bren looked the two jars over carefully. No glyphs! Then he had a terrible thought. What if there were more jars to be found in the temple of the wolf priests? Had he overlooked them in his hurry?

Bren sank to the floor by his father's bed, exhausted but struggling to decide what to do next.

Maybe he should get some sleep before going on. *Turn to page 40.*

Bren thought that he really didn't have the time to do more than rest and grab a bite to eat before continuing his quest. *Turn to page 9.*

Bren knew he had to take some time to eat and drink, but he begrudged every second. How could he waste even a minute resting while his father was dying?

Bren looked down at the magical amulet, not sure which icon to press next.

Maybe he should go back to the gnome and ask for more information. *Turn to page 41.*

Maybe he should return to the temple of the wolf priests and do some more hunting. *Turn to page 24.*

Bren suddenly found himself in darkness. "What is this?" he shouted. "I thought I was supposed to be sent home!"

"Did you really think it was going to be that easy?" The voice that boomed out of the darkness was cruel, cold, and definitely not human.

Darmu. It had to be Darmu. "I had a deal with your worshippers," Bren protested, trying not to let his sudden fear show. "I volunteered to be a sacrifice and was able to survive the test."

"What is that to me, little creature? I am Darmu, not some fool of a human! You and your father are still under my curse."

Bren thought of his father, the clever merchant who could talk people into almost anything. This was a good time to try his merchant skills. "There must be something you need that my father and I can give you," he said slowly. "Ah, yes, I have it. You haven't any temples in our country. Wouldn't it be useful to you if you had worshipers up north?"

"Do you think yourself able to accomplish what my southern clans have been unable to do for centuries?"

"My father and I are merchants. We can sell anything to anyone. Now let us strike a bargain," Bren continued, warming to the deal.

"If you dare."

"Let us live favored by you and we shall build a temple to you in the north. Your worship there will start out small, but with your power and glory I'm sure it will expand faster than any other faith in our land. Do we have a bargain?"

"I am no fool, little mortal. If I don't like what I see, you and yours will suffer as none has suffered ere now. Now *go!*"

Bren found himself instantly back at home, with his father cured of all ills. They should have been happy, but the dark shadow of Darmu hung over them. For the rest of their lives, they spent every day fearing the demon-god's wrath.

The End

That night, Bren, dressed in black clothes, kept to the shadows and easily avoided the night guard. The front of the temple was unguarded. He listened for a moment. Only the buzzing of insects could be heard. The moon and stars gave him more than enough light. Still keeping to the shadows, Bren entered the temple.

The inside of the temple was darker than the night outside, but enough moonlight filtered i⁻ to let Bren find the altar. He reached out for the Tomtek jar.

"Foolish mortal!" a voice boomed, and Bren nearly knocked the jar off the altar and had to grab at it to keep it from falling to the floor. "Why do you think there are no guards?"

Bren didn't care to answer that question. Such a vast, inhuman voice could only have come from the mighty war god Agar himself. Snatching up the jar, Bren ran for his life.

"Thunderbolts or lions, mortal, which is your death to be?" shouted the terrible voice.

In desperate defiance, Bren shouted back over his shoulder, "I pick old age!"

"Try to mock me, will you? Come into my house and take my things, will you? Bah, lions it is!"

There was a sudden savage roaring behind Bren. He glanced over his shoulder and saw large, tawny-yellow shapes gaining on him. Lions! Bren put on a new burst of speed, but the lions were faster. He felt hot breath on his back. Then he felt terrible claws sink into his shoulder, like red-hot knives, and the lion was pulling him over backwards.

Then that first and a second lion were upon him, fangs tearing at his flesh, powerful jaws crunching his bones. As he died in agony, Bren heard the booming voice of Agar say, "Well done, my kittens, well done. His foolish spirit will now spend all of eternity watching himself fail time and again to steal from me."

THE END

The walk to the tower tree of the owl spirit turned out to be almost alarmingly easy. Oh, yes, the forest was dark and the path was narrow and winding, little more than a deer track. But nothing attacked Bren, or even tried to stop him. It was a nice change, he thought.

He saw the massive tower tree long before he reached its trunk. Once he'd finally reached it, he called up, "Owl, are you up there? I need your help and advice. Please come out, just for a moment."

A blindingly white owl several times taller than Bren moved solemnly out on the thick branch of the tower tree. "Why do you bother me?" it asked.

"I've heard that you are wise," Bren said as politely as possible. "Please let me tell you my story."

"Speak."

Bren quickly told his story, growing more and more nervous during the telling. The owl never blinked and never stopped staring straight at Bren. Only when Bren was finished did the owl stir on his perch.

"Be pleased," the great bird said. "I have much good news to tell you. You and your father are no longer cursed. This land is favored by the gods and the second you stepped onto the grass here, you were freed of all harming magics. Also, worry not about returning your father's jars."

"Why is that, great owl?" Bren asked.

The massive owl spread its wings, soared down, and by way of answering Bren's question, ate him in two bites.

The End

As Bren headed down to the beach where the giant had said the storehouse was located, he heard the giant shouting, "Curse it all, sheep for lunch again!"

Now what did that mean? Maybe some food in the cave had spoiled.

Oh well, it wasn't important.

Bren discovered not one storehouse but four stone buildings, three of which were topped with bronze statues of athletes in the act of hurling javelins. The fourth building didn't have a statue on its roof, but there was a bronze statue of a warrior with shield and raised javelin a couple of hundred yards in the distance. A trail of footsteps led to the middle building and Bren saw that its door, also stone, was partially open. He couldn't budge it an inch wider, but he managed to squeeze inside.

This wasn't just a storehouse, it was a place of treasures, but treasures like no man had ever seen before. This, in fact, was a storehouse for giants. Huge golden hairpins lay atop pearl necklaces in which each pearl was larger than Bren's head. Giant crowns covered in enough large diamonds and rubies to buy all the buildings in Dragon City were lying on the floor by the hundreds, seemingly tossed into this corner or the other at random. Huge chests overflowed with gold and silver coins. Each coin was large enough for a grown man to have trouble lifting it. Pieces of giant-sized golden and platinum armor were everywhere. Huge javelins of gold and silver rested against the walls.

Then Bren cried out for joy as he saw them. There were at least ten Tomtek jars on an altar that sat at the top of a flight of thirteen tall stairs. Climbing those stairs was hard work for Bren, since each step was nearly taller than he was. But he managed to struggle his way up, finding small handholds in cracks and chips in the stone.

At the top of the stairs, Bren stood panting, struggling to catch his breath. But there in front of him was the altar. It was made of white marble carved with clouds. The heads of gods peaked through the clouds, and they were hurling lightning bolts down to the bottom of the altar.

All that mattered to Bren were the jars on top, and he quickly climbed the side of the altar, using the carvings as handholds, and started investigating each of the jars. Did any of them bear that mystic glyph?

No. There were no glyphs on them, and he couldn't really be sure they were from his father's collection.

Bren happened to glance up, and caught sight of his reflection in a mirror and scrambled back to his feet. He froze in shock. Oh, he didn't like what he saw, he really didn't like it. A dark shadow was moving all around his body. It looked almost like some type of nasty reptile. The snout of the demonic creature moved from one position on Bren's body to the next. It hurt Bren's eyes just to watch as it writhed all over him, even though he couldn't feel a thing. As he tried to grab pieces of the darkness, he grasped nothing. Clearly, he couldn't just pull the curse off like a piece of clothing. With a shudder, he turned away from the mirror.

Leaning against the back of the altar was a suit of gold armor—and what a suit it was. Bren climbed off the altar and checked out all the pieces. The armor was amazing. Just his size, it appeared to be made of solid gold, but each piece was as light as a feather. The breastplate had black and gold roses enameled all over it. The arm and leg greaves held carvings of stampeding unicorns. Bren might not be a warrior, but he knew enough about the art of the sword to recognize that the golden sword and its matching shield weren't just for show. They were powerful tools of war. He felt that if he used these, he'd walk a battlefield as strong and secure as a young god. But should he take them?

No one could possibly miss a few pieces of armor. He put it on and took up the sword and shield, then walked out, easily pushing open the door he couldn't budge just a few minutes ago. *Turn to page 97.*

His father was surely more important than treasure. Bren pressed an icon on the amulet. *Turn to page 87.*

Suddenly the idea of talking to the mayor seemed like a very good idea. Bren knocked hard on the mayor's door, hoping someone was there who would take his warning seriously.

"Come on in," a voice said.

To look at this strongly built man, Mayor Black was a farmer turned mayor. He stood, smiled, and offered his work-roughened hand.

Bren took it and sat down. "Mayor, my name is Bren of House Tawilden."

"Sorry, my boy, but that means nothing to me."

"I'm from Dragon City—"

"A long way off."

"Uh, yes. Now, I realize you don't know me, but I have to warn you that you have a problem. And I know this is going to be difficult for me to explain and for you to believe."

"Go ahead."

"There's a visitor, a sorcerer—I don't know what name he's using here, but his real title is the Sorcerer of Dex. And he's an evil man who plans on taking over your village."

The mayor stared at him in amazement. "Now, really, boy. That's a pretty fantastic story, and you're right that I can hardly believe what you're saying. Certainly not without more proof." He wrote something quickly on a shimmering sheet of paper, then waved the paper once in the air and it vanished in a puff of fire. As Bren stared at that, startled that the mayor knew any magic, the man added, "Tell me why you think this is the truth and why I should believe you."

Bren told him about all the historical facts he knew. There were the troll and ogre armies on both sides of the valley that would attack. There were the special entrances in the wall that the sorcerer had created.

Suddenly the door burst open.

"Thank you for calling me in, brother," said the Sorcerer of Dex. "Now who is this troublemaker bothering you, and where can I find him?"

Brother! Then there had been two evil sorcerers all along, not one. Bren stared at the mayor in horror.

It was the last thing he did, because at that moment, the mayor calmly cast a lightning bolt at him. As his spirit floated free, Bren thought sadly that history was indeed about to be repeated.

THE END

Bren hastily drew his sword. The sorcerer gave a sharp, scornful laugh.

"Very well, boy, let it be swords."

At his gesture, a sword formed in his hand—one that blazed with flames. Those had to be illusion, Bren thought. That had to be just an ordinary sword.

Whatever type of sword it was, the sorcerer was closing with him. The two blades clashed together. If it was illusion, Bren realized, it was a really good one, because he could feel the heat of those flames scorching his hands and face. The sorcerer was strong, too, and forced Bren back and back again.

But the sorcerer wasn't that good a swordsman, Bren realized. The man was using brute force rather than technique. Bren had been trained better than that. He pretended to lunge, and the sorcerer followed his lead, cutting left. Bren ducked right and lunged. The point of his sword stopped just short of stabbing through the sorcerer's throat.

"Now," Bren said, trying not to pant, "you are going to get me safely out of here. Not to Darmu, not to some trap, but safely out of here, do you understand?"

"Oh, I understand, all right. I also understand that you're a fool if you think you can defeat the Sorcerer of Dex so easily!"

Suddenly the hilt of Bren's sword was blazingly hot. He dropped it with a gasp of pain—but now he found himself completely enveloped in sorcerous fire. Bren screamed and tried to escape, but there was no escape. The flames burned his flesh and pulled the air from his lungs. As he felt the last life leave him, he heard the sorcerer say:

"What a shame. I'm afraid Darmu will have to live without meeting you."

THE END

Bren sat at home, running his father's merchant business and waiting. As the days passed, he did the accounting. He met with clients. There wasn't too much time to worry about his father. Now and then Bren wondered what was taking the men he'd hired so long to find even one of the jars. All too soon, the two weeks were almost up.

But no hired man ever returned. No jars were found. Bren sadly watched his father die. But at least the business was safe in his hands. His life would be long, safe, and boring. And he would forever be haunted by guilt.

The End

As the man-wolf lunged, Bren quickly drew his sword. But the wolf's bulk sent him crashing over backwards. Bren cut frantically sideways with his sword, but the blade merely glanced off the shoulder bone of the wolf. But Bren had his dagger in his other hand. It wasn't easy to do anything from this awkward angle. And the wolf was doing his best to get at Bren's throat. Desperately, Bren thrust his dagger up into the creature's open mouth—and on into its brain. The jaws clamped down on the handle of the dagger, and not Bren's throat. The man-wolf thrashed wildly for a moment, spraying blood all over, then shifted back to man-form and went limp.

It was dead. With one great heave, Bren managed to get the heavy body off him, then scrambled to his feet, shaking. He—he'd never killed a man before ... if that really had been a man ...

But others might come hunting for the priest. Sword in hand, Bren began searching the temple-tent, not sure what he was going to find. It was a maze of narrow, fur-lined walls, and he didn't dare get lost.

Turn to page 78.

Bren drew his sword and dagger. "I'm not going to give you my name," he told the dragon. "And I'm not going to let you eat me, either."

The dragon chuckled. "I can't tell you how many times I have heard that. And yet I have never once missed a dinner."

Bren took a step back, raising his sword. Those scales looked pretty tough, but if this was really an old dragon, there must be some that were broken or worn away.

He slashed—but the blade bounced off the blue scales, nearly pulling the sword from his hand. The dragon merely laughed, and batted at Bren with a clawed paw, sending the boy tumbling. The paw came down again, and Bren desperately lunged up with his dagger. The small blade lodged between two scales, and the dragon said, "Ouch! Naughty!"

But all it did was shake its paw, sending the dagger flying. The paw came crashing down on Bren. He was suddenly flattened against the floor, feeling bones crack but unable to yell because all the air had just left his lungs. Then the dragon's claws tightened, and Bren wished he *could* scream, because the pain of being crushed was horrible.

Worse, though, was knowing, in that last minute of blood and shattered bones, that he had failed himself and his father both.

The End

"I told those wolf priests, I told that wizard, and now I'm telling you, there is no teleporting allowed into the library," a voice squeaked from behind Bren.

Bren turned around with a shock. Glancing up, down, and all around, he found himself in the strangest library he'd ever seen. There were books and scrolls on shelves going all the way up the walls and crowded into every nook and cranny.

The protesting voice was attached to a small, green gnome in a plain brown suit. He shook a ruler at Bren.

"Please forgive my trespass," Bren said as politely as he could. "My father is dying and I'm questing in an attempt to save him, and I fear I haven't much time."

The gnome librarian listened and the anger left his face. "Well, well, well, that's quite a tale, youngster."

"You do believe me don't you?" Bren asked. "And do you have any idea how far I am from Dragon City?"

"Ooo, er, you're several thousand miles I should think. It's on another continent."

"Another ... continent," Bren echoed weakly. "How am I going to get home in time to help my father?"

"I could probably get you back home quite swiftly," the gnome said, "but we have a problem. The Tomtek jars we received yesterday are, a bit out of reach."

"I don't understand."

"Do you see that big, sturdy chest? A wizard cast a spell on it, and enchanted and might well bite you."

"Isn't there a way to open it?"

"There's only one key and the master librarian has it. Unfortunately, though, he is at a conference in another dimension and cannot be reached." The gnome held out a book. "Would you like to read while you wait?"

"I can't wait—my father can't wait!" Bren stared at the chest. "Can it chase me?"

"No," the gnome replied. "Its fangs can bite at you and its claws can animate to tear you to shreds, but it can't actually run." Bren began to form a plan.

Turn to 68.

Bren dreamed that he was climbing a mountain. He climbed for what felt like many hours and grew so tired he sat down on the path to rest. Then he fell asleep.

He woke with a shock, not sure if this was a dream or the real thing. He had rolled over the edge of the cliff and he was falling! Bren reached out frantically for any possible hold. He caught a handhold, but his fingers started to slowly slip. In another moment, he was going to fall to his death.

Someone was looking down at him from the top of the cliff. Who was it? The light was behind the figure, so Bren couldn't tell if it was a man or woman—or even a human being. "Help me!" he called. "Please, help!"

To his horror, the figure only laughed. It was definitely not a human laugh, deep and full of evil.

"Who are you?" Bren asked.

"Your enemy," the figure replied smoothly. "Yours and your father's, to be precise."

"Are you—you're the wolf priest's god!"

"Or demon, if you prefer. I am called Darmu. Oh, and yes, this is a dream, but if you die in it, you're not going to wake up again. Oh, and there you go, off the cliff's edge! Bye-bye, little human!"

As Bren fell, an image of his father dying in his bed flashed across his mind. He never should have stopped to sleep. Now it was too late for them both.

THE END

Bren faked a punch at the man nearest him. The man ducked, but that left an opening in the circle. Bren raced and dodged. He was going to get away!

Then the first spear hit him. Blazing pain shot through Bren, and he staggered. A second and a third spear struck, and Bren fell, struggling to get up. He drew one last gasp, choking on his own blood, then went limp.

Then he heard a voice, cold and full of malice. "Fool," it said, "now you'll feel my curse throughout all time!"

Then he ... wasn't dead? Or ... where was he?

Bren opened his eyes to find himself on the ground. Above him loomed a being whose eyes burned red. That was all Bren could tell. The rest was lost in darkness.

"Who are you?"

"I am Darmu," the being snapped. "It is my curse that raises you from the dead. My spirit rested among the other Tomteks in your father's home. I gave your family prosperity while you treated my spirit jar well. When it was stolen, you earned my curse. Begin your penance for foolishly losing my essence."

Bren found himself standing in the dinning room of his father's house. The wolf priests were loading jars into baskets while his father groaned on the floor, evil magics making his body jerk in spasms of pain.

The teenager cried out and knelt at his father's side. But Bren's hands went through his father's body.

The wolf priests made many trips with baskets filled with jars. Bren tried to stop them, but his hands and even his magical dagger had no effect.

Bren watched the priests leave in the night, laughing at their work. Going back to his father's body he called out to the gods in anguish. "What can I do?"

Suddenly, he found himself standing in the dining room again. The priests were putting the same jars in the same baskets. It was happening all over again.

Bren's eyes grew wide in terror as he puzzled out what he would be doing for all eternity.

THE END

As Bren turned with sword drawn, the monk cried out in surprise and alarm. He moved quickly, foot lashing out in a powerful kick. Off balance, Bren went over backwards—and fell right into the pentagram.

He was …

Oh no!

He was back in the wizard's deadly cellars. But there on the far side of the place he saw a Tomtek jar. There wasn't enough room for his sword, but Bren drew his dagger, knowing full well it could do little good against mold spores or fungus. But he had to have *some* weapon!

Trying not to breathe, he moved forward, but every step raised a cloud of spores. He stumbled to one knee, outspread hand stopping his fall but landing full on the fungi-covered floor. Scrambling up, Bren frantically rubbed the black, wet muck from his hand. His mind screamed in terror at the thought of all the possible poisons that might already be in his system. But he kept moving forward, aiming at the Tomtek jar, because that was all he could do.

Splashes of green jelly fungi fell from the ceiling as if it knew where he'd just been. Just as he reached for the jar, Bren heard several plops behind him and glanced up. The ceiling was all but boiling with rippling waves. That fungi somehow did know he was here. He had to get out of here, fast!

But sizzling green jelly fungus was all over the path he'd just taken.

Suddenly a tentacle swept out and grabbed him by the waist. The arm with the jar was pinned to his side, but his dagger arm was free. Bren stabbed down again and again against the flesh of the crushing tentacle that was dragging him steadily toward the wall on the far side of this chamber of horror. The dagger made wet sounds as it tore into the flesh of the tentacle. A sickening smelling green goo gushed out of the wounds he was making, nearly making him gag. But he kept stabbing away at the tentacle.

Then he saw the owner of the tentacle—something

flat against the wall but with a lot of tentacles, and one huge, fang-rimmed maw.

Bren gave up stabbing the tentacle and slashed with all his might at the creature's eyes. Black ichor spurted out, covering his dagger hand and arm in huge spurts. The monster roared in pain, and Bren desperately stabbed it again, with all his strength, right between its ruined eyes. He was tossed aside as the creature writhed, tentacles lashing. Then it fell limply aside, revealing the opening of what looked like the shaft of a mine.

Bren struggled back to his feet. He saw no mold or fungi on the bare earth floor of the shaft. But he wasn't going to make any hasty decisions. He looked back, where huge chunks of green jelly fungus were being hurled to the floor in a constant rain. Not good.

Bren quickly pressed an icon on the amulet. He had to get out of here, and fast! *Turn to page 72.*

That empty mine shaft looked pretty good to Bren compared to the green jelly fungus. *Turn to page 90.*

"Did you know you are cursed, boy?"

Bren opened his eyes to see an old warrior in red leather armor, his helm at his feet, sitting on a rock, sharpening a gladius. Everything else was in utter darkness.

"Where am I?" Bren asked.

"Why you're dead, boy. One of my worshipers killed you." The old warrior shrugged. "Normally, the curse you have on you would have sent you to watch yourself fail time and again for all eternity. I didn't much like that, since you did, after all, give yourself to my service."

"You are ... Agar, god of war?" Bren asked.

"That's me," the deity answered. "Normally I encourage my worshipers to kill nonbelievers, but you've caught me at a good time. A good time for you. too. I can't break the curse Darmu gave you, and if you don't know who he is, think demon god who isn't careful about the god part of it. What you did to get him so annoyed with you, I can't say. What I can do is give you a bit of justice. I'm sending your spirit back to before you made the bonehead mistake that got you here. Now be off with you, before I change my mind."

Turn to page 21.

"The answer to the riddle is 'both and neither,'" Bren said. "The deer owned it, but lost it to you. You didn't own it, but took ownership of it. Neither of you and both of you owned that heart."

"Well, I didn't expect *that* answer from you," the wolf said in surprise. "I won't eat you after all. Clever little creature, I'm going to send you to where you will find the rarest of your father's jars. They are in the possession of a rather ... interesting human. She's almost wolf-like."

Turn to page 81.

The gnome had been very specific about the where-abouts of this creature. He also said if Bren didn't talk about the creature's size that Bren should be fine talking to him … but forgot to mention the creature was a giant.

The giant was sprawled against the side of the mountain, napping peacefully by the mouth of his cave. He was wearing what looked like sewn-together sheep skins. It must have taken hundreds of sheep, Bren thought, to do the job. A huge club, twice the size of Bren, lay at the giant's side. In a sheltered little valley below the cave, a large herd sheep grazed. They obviously had no idea they were going to be turned into food or clothing.

"Excuse me! Hello!" Bren shouted up to the giant.

The giant grunted, then opened his eyes and slowly looked around. "Huh, who's there?"

"My name is Bren. I'm a merchant from Dragon City. Maybe you've heard of that place?" Bren asked casually.

"Never heard of it," the giant grunted. "I'm busy. Go away before I think about lunch."

The giant turned over, away from Bren.

"Just a moment more of your time," Bren pleaded. "Did you talk to any wolf priests about jars recently?"

"All right, all right, I'm up," the giant said. "And lunch it is." He raised his arms to stretch mightily. "Let's play a little game. I'll ask you a question and you give me the answer, and then you can ask a question of me. If either one of us doesn't like the answer we get, we are allowed to ask a second question right away."

The idea sounded like a good way to get information. Bren motioned for the giant to go first.

"About how tall are you and how much do you weigh?" asked the giant.

To Bren's mind that was two questions, but he wasn't about to quibble with a giant. "I'm about nine hand spans tall or seventy-two inches tall. I'm roughly nine stones or two hundred and twenty-five pounds in weight. Now, did the wolf priests offer you any jars and do you know where else they went on the island?"

Bren could ask multiple-part questions, too.

As Bren looked over the treasures just in the piles nearest him, he could see so many different types of riches that made his head swim. It would be foolish to try taking any of the gold coins or silver or gold bars he saw by the thousands all around him. That was just too much weight to carry, especially when there were so many more portable jewels and pieces of jewelry around for the taking. But what should he take? There were so many choices that it was almost overwhelming.

Should he take as many gems and lighter golden objects as he could carry? *Turn to page 89.*

Should he look over the pile more carefully for the most unusual objects? *Turn to page 83.*

Bren woke slowly. He was lying on something soft ... a carpet ... his father's carpet, his father's house! There was no sign of Darmu. Had the demon been destroyed with his essence? And ... had the curse been removed?

He scrambled to his feet, about to race up the staircase to his father's bedroom. But his father came hurrying down the stairs, full of health, and caught his son in his arms.

The curse was gone forever.

The End

Bren hesitated. Darmu was a demon, and that meant that anything he said might be a lie. His word could never be trusted.

All right then, Bren thought, to fight Darmu, he wouldn't be a warrior, he'd be a merchant, or maybe a warrior-merchant. Able to fight, that was, but cunning as well.

"You must be bored," he said to Darmu.

The red eyes blinked in surprise. "What nonsense is this?"

"You're a demon, a powerful being. Why would you waste your time with two little mortals like my father and me?"

"Do you dare to question me?"

"I'm not questioning anything," Bren said smoothly. "Just wondering."

The longer he kept Darmu talking, the longer he was safe, and the more time he had to come up with a real plan.

"I do what pleases me," Darmu said, and there was chill menace in his voice. "And you *are* beginning to bore me."

Bren decided on a surprise attack. *Turn to page 73.*

Bren was sure that the demon was hiding something. *Turn to page 59.*

Tired and aching with worry, Bren sat wearily on the edge of a fountain. Oh yes, he'd managed to recover a few of the jars, since those in the city who did collect Tomtek jars were honest men and women who didn't want to keep stolen property. But the returned jars hadn't made a change in his father's condition. There were still jars missing—including that special one.

By now, Bren had gone over almost the whole city, but no one else in all of Dragon City seemed to know anything about stolen jars. Still, he realized suddenly, there was one collector he hadn't tried. This was someone named Achernso, a foreigner new to the city who was said to collect Tomtek jars. Bren headed off to speak with him.

Achernso was a tall, lean, cold-eyed man. He stood in the doorway of his house, flanked by two muscular guards, and didn't invite Bren inside. He listened to Bren's story without even blinking.

"You have to understand," Bren tried again. "My father is very sick. He might die! Last night evil priests robbed him of his collection of Tomtek jars. The only way to save his life is to find one of these jars and return it. You collect Tomtek jars—"

"Are you accusing me of being a thief?"

"No, sir. I just want to see the jars—"

"No."

"But it won't take long."

"I said no! Go look for those wolf priests if you're so worried."

"I'm not accusing you of anything!" Bren argued. "All I need to do is look at the jars!" He tried to push past Achernso.

"Guards!" Achernso shouted.

Before Bren could move, the two burly men caught him by the shoulders and threw him out onto the street. As he lay in the dust, trying to catch his breath, the door slammed shut behind him. He heard heavy bolts dropping into place.

Great. Now he had to either find another way into

Achernso's manor, or take his suggestion and go after the wolf priests.

Bren decided to go after the priests of the wolf god. *Turn to page 64.*

Bren needed to see inside Achernso's manor. The only way past those guards was to slip in like a thief. *Turn to page 93.*

"Ah, and once again you prove yourself a fool!" a cold voice said out of the darkness. "Do you know how many times you have died on this quest?"

Bren saw two eerie green spots of light. Eyes, he thought. The eyes of ... of ... what?

"Who are you?" he asked. "Where am I?"

"Where you are, little thing, is dead. And who I am is your deepest, most terrible of foes. Know that I am Darmu."

Suddenly Bren knew this had happened before. Suddenly he knew this was the dark god who had cursed his father—and himself—for owning Darmu's Tomtek jar. All he could do now was shiver in fear.

"What, no questions?" Darmu taunted. "You have tried and failed this quest hundreds of times. Now I'll be sending you back to watch how you and your father stupidly die over and over again for all eternity. Now go."

The End

The teenager rushed back up the stairs and burst into the wizard's chamber. The spell caster scowled at him.

"Great and powerful wizard," Bren pleaded. "Please have mercy on me and my father. There is no way to reach my father's jar without my being killed. Please with all your power, you could easily give me the jar. I'm begging you to help me." Bren fell to his knees.

"Ah, so you are a coward after all. What a shame. Know that I go down to that room every day and the tentacles of the wall and the slimes of the ceiling bother me not at all. Go back to the wolves."

Before Bren could get to his feet, the wizard reached out and pressed an icon on the amulet.

Turn to page 44.

Bren was sure that if he didn't get some sleep, he wasn't going to be able to survive whatever dangers would face him. Throwing a blanket down at the foot of his father's bed, he settled down for the night.

Turn to page 22.

When Bren asked the gnome if he knew anything about the wolf priests, the gnome said, "Why, yes! I know of them. They were here, as a matter of fact, and went to talk with several people on the island on which this library rests. Then I do believe that they left."

Bren thought that he'd better go talk to those people as well. *Turn to page 70.*

The icon of the wolf on the mountain caught his attention. *Bren pressed that. Turn to page 45.*

Bren sheathed his weapons, knowing they would do nothing against the tough blue scales of the dragon. Imitating his father working a good deal, he asked smoothly, "Would you be interested in striking a bargain with me for your pet's Tomtek jar? I could offer you a great deal."

The dragon chuckled. "Now what could a nice little snack such as you possibly offer me?"

"You won't know unless you ask," Bren countered.

"There's a bit of magic in the jar," explained Garyant. "The power of that jar is making my little friend healthier than it ever was before. I will only ask you one more time, what is your name, human, and what do you think you have that would interest an old dragon like me?"

Bren thought faster than he'd ever thought before. "What do you eat?"

"Huh, that's an odd question," the dragon replied. "Monsters come into my tunnels all the time. If I wanted to, I could always force my body out into the skies, but I'm a bit too lazy right now to do that."

"Have you ever eaten cows or sheep?" Bren said warming to the trade talks.

The dragon licked its fangs. "All dragons love the taste of sheep and cows."

"You never asked me for the name of my city, but I'll tell you. It's Erehwon. Got that? Now, in Erehwon I have a bit of money. You let me go now, and twice a year for two years, this will happen. In the summer, I'll drive a herd of sheep into your cave. In the winter, I'll drive a herd of cows. So, now. Do we have a bargain?"

The dragon backed off a bit and put its huge head down on the cavern floor. Its eyes, two great black circles, were now even with Bren's head. "You do realize I will come and destroy your city if you don't deliver the herds for four years, don't you?"

Bren gulped feeling the dragon's hot breath on his entire body. But he thought, *If you can find a city that's "Nowhere" backwards, you can do what you want to it!* "Do we have a deal at four years?"

The dragon reached out and plucked the jar from the body of the still struggling blob of flesh.

"Little Artool can do without its toy," the dragon said. "I look forward to the delivery of cows. If the land is covered in snow and the cows aren't here. I'll find you. Your scent is quite unique."

Bren snatched up the jar. "Yes, well, thanks, I think. I'll get your cows as soon as I can. It's a bargain you won't regret."

"Hmmmm, yes, I know," the dragon was almost purring. "You'd better go before I change my mind."

Don't worry, Bren thought, *I'm out of here.*

But where should he go?

Bren didn't dare waste a second. He pressed the first icon he could touch, the largest, the pentagram. *Turn to 106.*

Bren thought he'd better go straight home—assuming that the icon he'd first pressed took him there. But when he pressed it, he was astonished that it had taken him back to the wolf priests' temple. *Turn to 44.*

Bren ran—but he had forgotten how fast a wolf can move. In one mighty bound, it was between him and the outer wall of the tent. It laughed at him, an eerie, inhuman sound coming from the sharp-fanged mouth. Bren turned and headed for what looked like a narrow maze of fabric walls. Maybe he could lose the wolf in there.

But it wasn't the only one. Two more wolves came out of openings in the fabric, laughing at him. He was trapped! Bren whipped out his sword, but the wolves lunged as one. Powerful jaws closed on his sword arm, and Bren cried out in agony as the bones were crushed. Another set of jaws closed on his legs, tearing the flesh to the bone, and Bren screamed. Then the third set of jaws closed on his throat. Drowning in his own blood, Bren knew too late that he and his father were both doomed. Then he knew nothing at all.

The End

"You've come earlier than expected, young lord," a tranquil voice said. "But welcome."

Bren looked about, trying to orient himself. He was standing on a steep mountainside bathed in the reddish light of the setting sun. Before him sat an orange-robed, shaven-headed monk in a lotus position—one who was floating several feet off the ground.

There in front of him was a Tomtek jar.

"I'm no lord, just a merchant's son," Bren said. "My father had Tomtek jars stolen from him. I have to ask if that jar is from his collection."

"Please excuse my small deception," replied the monk. He waved a hand, and the jar disappeared. "That illusion was necessary in order to bring you here to our temple." With a wave of his hand, he pointed into the mountains and there, just a speck in the distance was what looked like a red-walled structure high, high in the mountains. "Many Tomtek jars are up there. All you have to do to get those is climb the path and make a choice when you get to the temple."

The monk himself then vanished. He'd been an illusion, too. Not knowing what else to do, Bren started up the steep path into the mountains. It wasn't easy, but at least he didn't have to do any real mountain-climbing. It was just a long way up.

Panting and exhausted after a climb of what had seemed like hours, Bren finally reached the huge bronze doors of the temple.

How do I get in? Just, uh, knock?

Turn to 123.

Bren was led to the edge of the river. Many of the men and women went with him. They were all grinning and jesting among themselves. Bren didn't think he liked the festive atmosphere.

He looked out at the river. The current looked pretty swift, but he thought he could manage that. But then Bren saw several large crocodiles on a sand bar in the middle of the river, lazing in the noon day sun. Oh yes, it wouldn't be a difficult dive—if those monsters would leave him alone. He was pretty sure that they wouldn't.

He was also pretty sure that he wouldn't get a chance to back out of this.

Bren began to strip, keeping on only his dagger on its narrow belt, then paused. "I could just ignore your god, you know. I could just choose to not risk my life for your cruel amusement, and leave."

"You would be killed before you went three steps," Garlun-ta replied.

Bren shrugged. "The worshiper who killed me while your god's curse was on me would surely anger your god and be cursed as well."

"What do you want?" Garlun-ta asked angrily.

"Take the curse off my father and me," Bren answered quickly. "Surely one who has the favor of Darmu can easily do this. When the curse is lifted from both of us, I'll dive in and take my chances. You get what you want and I'll be sure my father is alive. Do we have a deal?"

"I cannot speak for the mighty Darmu. Cease this delay, or die now."

Well, it had been worth a try. Not expecting to live more than a few heartbeats. Bren dove into the river. Briefly he thought about just swimming over to the other side of the river and making a break for it. No. Not with those crocodiles waiting on the sand bar. Better to get that sacred stone and ... hopefully ... make it to the shore again.

At least the water was clear enough for him to see the sacred stone, which had a spiral glyph carved onto it. He just might be able to make a straight dive to it, then a straight swim to the shore before the crocodiles could get him. Bren made that straight dive, got the stone, and then started the swim back.

Unfortunately, one monster of a crocodile dove off the sandbar and began swimming almost lazily after him.

Bren turned to fight the crocodile. *Turn to page 116.*

Bren figured he'd try to get to shore. *Turn to page 79.*

Bren returned to the temple and handed a silver coin to the first priest he met. "Please take that as a donation to your temple. Could you tell me where I could find the leader of your priesthood?"

The priest smiled. "That would be Forceleader Donal. He's at the front portal welcoming worshipers this morning."

The Forceleader was a tall, broad-shouldered man who clearly had seen battle before he'd become a priest. He listened to Bren's story without comment.

"Please let me take the jar back to my father's house," Bren finished. "I'll replace it with another of its type, I swear it."

The Forceleader shook his head. "This jar has already been consecrated to Agar. The only way you could possibly gain it now is to fight to the death as a sacrifice to our god. If you should win, you would be allowed to take the jar."

Without a second thought, Bren said, "I'll do it."

"On your head be it, boy." Forceleader Donal gestured to one of the warriors, then took the pair to the center of the temple. There was a large circle worked in red mosaic. The Forceleader proclaimed, "You will fight to the death for the greater glory of Agar. If either one of you is forced out of the circle, you will be killed. Neither one of you may beg for quarter. The winner walks out with the glory of our god enfolding him all his days. Begin!"

Bren knew he was a pretty good swordsman, but he also knew he wasn't a trained warrior—his opponent was. The warrior-priest rushed Bren, anticipated the boy's dodge to the right, and thrust his gladius up into Bren's chest. Stunned with the sudden agony, Bren stood helpless for a moment, feeling his heart's blood pouring out. Then his legs gave way under him and he fell. Darkness came over him.

Turn to page 28.

"The heart is the deer's," Bren said, "no matter when it's taken from its body. It made it, it used it, and the fact that you ripped it away from the deer can't change that."

"Wrong answer, my next meal." The mammoth body of the wolf spirit emerged from the cave. "I'll allow you a few more heartbeats to live. I won't begin chasing you until the sun touches the horizon. Now run, my little tidbit!"

Bren didn't need to be told twice. He only wished he knew the land better. He leapt down the mountainside and dove into the forest. There was an hour or maybe a bit more before the sun set. It was already dark in the forest, though, and he stumbled over roots and got hit by branches as he ran. His legs ached, his lungs burned, and his heart was pounding so hard he was sure it was trying to get out.

At last he had to stop, bent over, panting. Around him, the night was coming in, but at least he didn't hear any wolf howls yet, or the sounds of anything heavy coming after him.

"Hello there, mortal man," said a sweet voice from somewhere above him.

He straightened with a gasp and looked up an oak tree to where a lovely woman sat on a branch. Slim and green-eyed, with skin that was an odd but attractive greenish-tan, she was dressed in a smooth, sleek gown that looked like it was made of oak leaves. She dropped lightly from the branch on which she'd been perching, and her bright smile stopped him dead.

"My, you are a handsome one of your kind." She circled him, still smiling. "The spirits of this forest call me Druas. What's your name, handsome one?"

"I'm, uh, Bren of, uh, House Tawilden." Fear was trying to drive him on, but her loveliness held him in place. "The wolf spirit plans on eating me. I must run."

Druas took his hands in hers. Hers were soft as silk, but with an unexpected strength hiding behind the softness. "Oh, don't worry about that bad old wolf," she purred. "He's just an overgrown puppy. Come to my home in the oak. No one will bother you there. You and I have many things to … discuss." Then she kissed him ever so softly on the lips.

The kiss instantly wiped out all fear, all memory. Bren followed her happily and thoughtlessly into her oak. As it closed about him, he had only one moment of worry. But then Druas kissed him again, and all worry left his mind. He dimly heard her coo, "Ah, nice little slave, you'll be here serving me forever."

Then he stopped thinking.

Forever.

The End

The giant came out of his cave with a sigh. "No luck. Flour's definitely all gone. Tell me, Bren, did you like getting your jars back?"

"Yes, and thank you very kindly for that," Bren replied.

"And if you don't mind my asking, did I tell you everything you wanted to know?" the giant asked with an expectant look on his face.

"Yes you did," Bren said. "And I have to say that your vegetable soup smells really good." Bren smiled up into the happy face of the giant.

"Oh, I'm not having vegetable soup," said the giant, stirring the boiling mixture. He paused. "This is an odd question, I know, but could you take off your shirt? There's some type of evil magic I'm sensing on your body, and it's centered on your back. It's very possible those evil priests laid a curse on you and I think I'm sensing it."

Bren quickly stripped off his things. "My father and I are both cursed. What do you see?" Bren asked as he turned his back toward the giant.

"I see a foolish young mortal all prepared for lunch!" the giant roared. He grabbed the surprised Bren and shoved him head first into the boiling water of the kettle. The last thing Bren heard as he boiled to death, was the giant saying, "I think you'll find, young and tender human, that boiling in soup removes most curses."

THE END

The spell caster must be evil. Bren doubted the being he faced was even human. Moving as quietly as he could, he drew his dagger, then threw it at the wizard.

The dagger stopped in mid air. "You won't appreciate this," the wizard said, getting to his feet, "but it's devilishly difficult to stop an enchanted dagger in mid-throw."

Bren took a step back in shock.

"I needed the practice actually," the wizard continued, "so I'm glad you decided not to take me up on my offer." He walked all around the dagger suspended in the air, clearly admiring his work.

"And now, let's take care of you, boy. I don't think I'll kill you after all."

A muttered word, and suddenly, Bren was looking way up at the huge wizard in the huge chamber.

"Yes, I was right," the wizard said with a cold smile. "You do make a fine-looking frog. Enjoy your new life, froggie. You'll forget you once were human soon enough."

With that, he tipped the frog who had been Bren out a window into a pond.

THE END

To Bren's relief, he saw that he had successfully returned to the gnomish library.

"Oh dear. You again," the gnome said. "Want me to send you home, do you?"

"Yes, thank you, I do."

True to his word, the little gnome magically sent Bren back home. As his senses cleared, Bren saw his father sleeping, and heard a little shriek from the neighbor lady who had been sitting with him.

"It's just me, Ma'am Elinai. Don't worry. I'm just here to catch my breath. I'll be going again soon."

Suddenly, a human eye the size of a head appeared in the chamber and started looking over everything. Someone was magically spying on them! Bren stabbed at the eye with his dagger—and someone yelled in pain at the back of the house. Bren rushed out the back door, weapons drawn and shouting, "Alarm, alarm!" to alert the neighbors.

But the neighbors were already alerted. Bren heard someone shout, "Kill the bloody priests! These are the ones who hurt Tawilden."

Bren found seven wolf priests, all dressed in their black leather. Two of them were already down on the ground with their skulls bashed in. Bren joined his trusty neighbors in the battle, and he wasn't going to let any of the wolf priests escape.

The priests were doing their best to throw magic spells and were using their wolf staves on the growing crowd. More and more neighbors and people of the other merchant guilds were coming to see what the noise was all about. None of them liked the wolf priests and soon there was a battle royal going on in the streets behind Bren's villa.

Bren found himself fighting a large, powerfully-built priest. Bren couldn't get in a telling blow since the wolf staff blocked every move he made. Then the priest started muttering something in a strange language, and Bren fell back, suddenly very dizzy. A savage blow from the staff struck him in the head and knocked him to the ground.

Before he could recover, another blow smashed down on the back of his skull. Darkness filled his mind.

He woke up in the middle of the battle, but all was strangely calm around him. He was looking down at his body.

"I'm sorry, son," the spirit of his father said. "The gods have claimed our bodies. Now Darmu's curse will make us walk the many paths of reality forever."

THE END

Bren moved toward the side caves and felt immediately better. That mass of loose gold towering above his head and ending with a dragon on top, had been too much danger for him to handle. He headed down a tunnel to a small cavern filled with weapons and armor.

"Pick me up," shouted a voice from the pile of swords in front of him.

"Mortal, you would be much better served by picking me up," said another voice.

"Magical weapons are all very well and good, but it's clear to me you need a magical shield to protect you," said a deep voice among the shields in the far corner of the room.

"Talking equipment," Bren said, marveling at what he was hearing. "Please don't fuss over me. I'll come back for several of you, but I can only carry so much. Let me explore the other caverns first."

"That's very wise of you, young man," said a very deep voice from the piles of armor at the center of the chamber. "I believe you'll find some magical carrying sacks and backpacks in the third chamber along."

Bren thanked all the voices and moved on, filled with wonder.

More tunnels led to another chamber. This time the area was filled with clothing. Some of the silky hats floated in the air. Several pairs of boots started hopping toward him. While he was curious, he didn't dare put them on as he'd heard stories of people being driven to their death from exhaustion by dancing boots.

Two of the cloaks floated up and Bren came into the room as if they offered themselves to him. Bren approached a strange cloak hanging from a silver pole, and couldn't resist touching the satiny material. At first the cloak looked solid black, but Bren's hand made the cloth shimmer, and silvery faces started appearing in the folds. Each face was contorted in horror. Bren dropped the cloak in shock, but the faces continued to shimmer and shift in the cloth. He started to hear tiny voices.

"Free me for the love of the gods."

"It's cold here, let me go, please."

"My family needs me, please, please let me be free."

"I—I can't, I'm sorry, I don't know how."

Bren ran from the room. He knew that cloak must be more terrible than the curse that lay on him. There were souls trapped in that cloak. Overcome with horror, he hurried into the next set of tunnels, not watching where he was going.

It was a foolish mistake. Monstrous centipedes dropped down on him from an overhang. Their great weight crushed him to the cavern floor, and their terrible mandibles cut into him, nipping him apart. As he died screaming, his spirit was dragged from its body.

"Mortal, you've been cursed by the powerful Darmu," one demonic creature said.

"My father!"

"It doesn't matter what wish you might have made to save your father," said another creature. "We still have you. And you are still going to suffer. We are taking you to the great Darmu, and once there, you are going to be one of his spirit slaves for all eternity."

The End

Wonderstruck, Bren walked around the tower. The structure was huge, and looked as thought it had been cut from one gigantic crystal. Looking up and down and all around the tower, Bren could see no windows, and just one door. The door alone was not made of crystal, but of wood sheathed in steel.

He hesitantly knocked. No one answered. Warily, Bren tried the door. It opened smoothly, soundlessly, and Bren, after a quick glance around for traps, entered. To his surprise, he found himself in a very pleasant chamber, like something that might be found in a wealthy man's home, with comfortable couches, a nicely blazing fire in a crystal fireplace, and shelves full of scrolls and books lining the walls. A table held food and drink, and the small cakes he saw resting on crystal plates smelled wonderful. A staircase wound up to a second floor.

As he stepped further into the room, the door slid shut behind him. Bren turned to discover a bare wall of smooth crystal where the door should have been.

Turn to page 91.

Something wasn't right about all this, Bren thought. There was no reason for a powerful demon like Darmu to be so determined to curse not a god but two small, relatively unimportant mortals ...

Unless Darmu wanted something from them? From him..? Unless Darmu *meant* for Bren to come to him?

Unless Darmu needed him for something.

Bren's eyes had finally adjusted to what little light there was. And he could have sworn he saw a familiar white shape there beside the great bulk of Darmu.

"A Tomtek jar!" Bren cried. "Yes, of course it is—it's *your* jar, isn't it?"

"Is it?"

"I was right, wasn't I? This whole thing, this curse, this quest, everything from the theft on to now, it was all a deliberate plan to get me here!"

"Clever little mortal. Can you guess why?"

"Something to do with my father ... or me ... Oh. That's it. That has to be it. You didn't just want us to keep it safe for you. No, it was you who ordered it stolen and brought here to you. You want it opened, don't you? That has to be what you want. And you, for all your power, can't do it!"

"Too many humans have handled it!" Darmu roared. "Your father and you the last among them. Your human auras surround it and block me!"

"That's too bad," Bren said dryly.

"For you!" the demon returned in fury.

Invisible flame engulfed Bren. He fought wildly to escape the terrible heat, but there was no escape. Then, just as suddenly, they were gone, leaving him staggering.

"You—you want me to open the jar, don't you?" he gasped. "Your essence is—trapped in it, isn't it?"

"Open the jar!" Darmu thundered.

"No."

The flames returned, more terrible than before. Bren knew they couldn't be real, he knew they had to be illusion—but they hurt so much! He couldn't even think! He fell to his knees, struggling not to scream. Dimly, he heard Darmu rant: "It was the gods who tore my essence from me, the gods who sealed it in that jar. When my essence is freed, then shall I be all powerful! Then shall all the world, all the heavens bow down to me!"

The flames vanished. Bren huddled on the floor, too worn to stand.

"Open the jar." This time, Darmu's voice was almost reasonable.

About to refuse again, Bren paused. A faint idea stole into his numb brain. Why was Darmu insisting that the jar be opened? No broken, opened.

"Open the jar," Darmu repeated more insistently. "Open it."

"Yes," Bren said.

"Ah, splendid, little thing! I was growing bored with flames."

Bren somehow managed to get to his feet. He stumbled forward, determined. This time he wasn't going to let illusion stop him. There was a way to block it ...

Two times one is two. Two times two is four. Two times three is six ...

The multiplication tables were basic, elemental. They were drummed into every merchant's mind from childhood. And their solid logic left no room for illusion.

Bren picked up the jar.

"Yes, yes!" Darmu urged. "Open it!"

His demonic will beat at Bren's mind. Grimly, Bren continued, *Two times four is eight ...*

Bren raised the jar over his head.

"No!" Darmu shrieked.

Two times five is ten, two times six is twelve ...

Bren brought the jar crashing down to the floor. As it shattered, Darmu screamed. A small, slimy thing like a jet-black, oily worm wriggled out of the shards—

But Bren stomped on it with all his might. The darkness erupted into a whirlwind.

Turn to page 34.

Bren had appeared on the edge of a large, flat area—a practice field, he realized after a moment, one of several, on which warriors were performing different kinds of martial arts in front of a large white building. A temple, perhaps? It was plain, without ornament, a very businesslike building, but a war god wouldn't want frills.

To his right, men in armor threw javelins at man-shaped targets, rarely missing, while to his left, other warriors drilled in formation. Before the building itself, warriors dueled with practice swords. Still other men sharpened swords and fixed armor at blacksmith forges.

Bren approached one of the resting warriors. "Can anyone go in the temple?"

The man looked up at Bren, clearly impatient with the question. "Another of you green recruits! Don't they teach you anything? Yes, yes, our god will smile on anyone, even boys like you with toothpicks for weapons."

Now deliberately ignoring Bren, the man went back to watching the practice.

Bren went up the steps of the temple two at a time. It was a large structure, but it was still designed in the fashion of most of the temples he'd seen: There was a big inner chamber where services to the god were held. On an altar made of bound shields were several ceramic bowls and statues—and a Tomtek jar.

Bren started towards the altar, but a warrior-priest dressed in red robes and wearing a sword blocked his path. "Sorry, recruit. No one but priests are allowed near the holy altar."

"I'm sorry. I'm just curious about that Tomtek jar."

The priest beamed. "Handsome, isn't it? That lion head makes a perfect icon."

"Could I get a closer look at it?"

The good humor vanished from the priest's face. "No. You cannot. Only priests may touch the altar. Now, is there something else I can help you with?"

Bren tried again. "I didn't say it very well. My family owned the jar and it was stolen from us. I need that jar back and I'll pay in gold for it. Would that be possible?"

The priest shook his head. "It's been given to our god of war. What kind of priest would I be if I allowed someone to take the things of our god?"

"What if I can prove that jar belonged to my father?" Bren asked.

"I'm telling you it doesn't matter who that jar belonged to in the ancient past or just yesterday," the priest all but growled at Bren. "It's been dedicated to the mighty Agar. I told you, only a priest may even approach it. Now be off with you!"

Bren knew he wasn't going to get anywhere with this priest. He walked away thinking about his options.

Bren decided to go back to the temple that night and see if this was the right jar. If it was, he'd just take it. Surely he could outrun any guard. *Turn to page 11.*

Bren thought that maybe other priests would actually listen to him and just give him his jar back. *Turn to page 48.*

The temple of the wolf god stood outside Dragon City's gates. It turned out not to be a solid building, but an enormous tent covered with wolf pelts, sitting on a platform with hundreds of metal wheels. The wolf priests could move it wherever they thought there might be a chance to preach and win supporters.

Sure. Or steal Tomtek jars, Bren thought.

There was just enough moonlight to let Bren see where he was going—and to realize to his surprise that there didn't seem to be any guards. He tiptoed forward. He wasn't going to try walking boldly into the main entrance, but it was easy to slip onto the platform and under one edge of the tent.

Too easy? Or were the wolf priests so sure that no one would bother them? Bren got to his feet and looked about. It was dark in here, with only one torch providing any light.

"We knew you would come here," a voice said in the darkness.

Bren nearly let out a started yelp. But he managed to say in a voice that was almost calm, "Show yourself."

A muscular man in red robes and black leather armor stepped into the torch light. "Ah yes. The boy. We suspected you would come here like a thief in the night."

"A thief?" Bren exclaimed. "Me? You're the ones who stole my father's jars, yes, and cursed us."

The priest gave a harsh laugh. "Those jars were stolen from us centuries ago, and we needed them back. Our order will now grow great again with the returned spirit power of our wolf gods."

"If you have the jars you claim are yours, why did you curse us?"

"We didn't curse you. Great Darmu spoke through us, cursing you for allowing a certain jar to be stolen. I don't know which jar it was, and I care not." He shrugged. "The other jars we sold."

"There aren't that many people in all the world wanting such a collection!"

The noise the priest made sounded like the growl of

a wolf. "We didn't sell to people. Great powers wanted many of those jars, and our magic sent the jars to them." His smile was a wolf's snarl. "Did you wonder why you saw no guards? We need none. You are as cursed as your father, but you won't know just how cursed you are until after I kill you!"

The priest dropped to hands and knees, growling—and suddenly became a huge wolf.

Bren didn't want to fight a wolf. He decided to get out of there, fast. *Turn to 44*.

Bren had to know if the special Tomtek jar was here. That meant fighting the wolf. *Turn to 19*.

As the guard entered, Bren slipped behind him. Picking up a heavy paperweight, he raised it over his head. But then he hesitated. He'd never done anything like this before. What if he hit the man too hard? What if he killed him? The guard was only doing his job, after all.

Bren had hesitated a little too long. Suddenly the guard whirled, catching Bren's arm in a powerful grip.

"Drop it, kid. I said, drop it!"

Bren didn't have a choice. He let the paperweight fall. "I'm not a thief," he protested. "I'm here to see about stolen property."

"Sure you are."

"I mean it! Those jars were stolen from my father, and I—"

"That's for Lord Achernso to decide."

Bren thought he might be able to pull free and escape. *Turn to page 85.*

Bren knew he might not get a better chance to talk with Achernso, so he went along with the guard. *Turn to page 11.*

Bren had no intention of leaving this place without his father's Tomtek jar, assuming that there was one here. If there was, he'd be willing to make any deal he could. He took a wary step out of the pentagram, but then stopped with a gasp, feeling a sudden alarming tightening about his chest. It felt as though someone was tightening a band of steel about him.

"That crush you're feeling is one of my invisible servants," the wizard said, smiling. "If I wish, it will kill you, but I'm willing to be reasonable. Drop that amulet on the table and I'll let you leave."

Grasping at straws, Bren gasped out, "The curse could harm you as well. A god was in one of those jars."

The wizard frowned, then gestured, and the crushing weight lifted from Bren's chest. Gasping, Bren quickly moved behind a large table with lots of magical items on it. Maybe the wizard wouldn't kill him when so much mage equipment was at stake.

"Not there, clever young man," the wizard said. "Come around the table and tell me how a merchant boy knows about curses and gods in Tomtek jars."

The truth, or at least most of it, Bren thought, was the only thing that would save him. "I know nothing of magic," he began, carefully moving around the table. "But the healer I got for my father told me about the curse and the need to get the jars back. It may well be that the spirit of a god rested in one of the jars. The god plainly didn't like being removed from my dad's shelves. It cursed my father and myself." Trying to keep eyes and face utterly innocent, Bren continued, "If you have one of the magical jars, the god could get mad at you as well."

The wizard, clearly annoyed with the whole situation, said, "Oh, I truly doubt it. But there is a Tomtek jar down in my cellars. If you can deal with my guardian, you can take back your jar. Mind you, boy, the guardian will eat you if you've lied to me. Follow the light sprite down to the cellars. Don't touch anything along the way or you may get eaten sooner than you expected. Be gone!"

The wizard gestured and muttered something, and a large spark of light appeared. The spark began moving past Bren, clearly meant to show him the way. The wizard turned his back on Bren and went back to his experiments as though he was alone.

Bren couldn't help testing. He started over to one of the shelves, but before he could touch anything, the wizard, without turning around, snarled, "Don't, or I really must kill you."

That settled it. The wizard knew exactly where he was without having to look. The light sprite was bouncing up and down by a staircase as if telling Bren to come with it, now!

But there was no way to know if the wizard was telling the truth. And it had, after all, been the wizard who had made the amulet for the wolf priests.

Bren decided to risk attacking the wizard. *Turn to page 102.*

Bren didn't think he had much of a choice. He accepted the wizard's word, and headed down to the cellars. *Turn to page 127.*

"Does the chest know of the valuable items it holds?" Bren asked.

"Oh yes, it's very aware of what it guards," the gnome answered. "That's part of its magic. One opens the chest and the chest tries its best to guard the items."

Bren knelt just out of biting range of the chest, or what he hoped was out of range. He made a big show of protecting what could have been a Tomtek jar but was actually his bundled-up pack. "Your key isn't here right now," Bren said directly addressing the chest. "But we have another jar that only you can guard. It's just like the ones you have now. It needs to be guarded, it really does."

Behind him, Bren heard the gnome gasp in surprise as the chest opened its fanged lid. Inside, he saw several jars. Were these from his father's collection?

"Thank you, chest," Bren said soothingly. "Just let me put this jar inside you as you keep your ... powerful ... sharp-jawed ... lid open."

While the jaws were open, the eyes of the chest couldn't see to the front. Bren pretended to put a jar into the chest, but he was actually checking the other jars for the telltale glyphs ...

No glyphs. The jar he must have wasn't here. Bren stood up with a sigh, and the chest crashed shut. He and the gnome left the chamber.

"That was amazing, just amazing," the gnome exclaimed. "It was worth watching just to know there is a trick to make the chest open without its key. Would you like to sit and read awhile to recover after that little adventure? We do have quite a few fascinating scholarly texts."

"Uh, no thank you."

"I understand. Then would you like me to transport you to your home?"

It was tempting. But maybe the gnome librarian, with all this knowledge around them, had some useful information.

Bren decided to take up the librarian's offer and go home. *Turn to 7.*

Bren thought that he'd better gather more information before even thinking about going home. *Turn to 41.*

Following the gnome's instructions, Bren pressed an icon on the amulet, one of the ones with a figure he couldn't quite make out. He found himself instantly in the middle of a hot, steamy forest, staring up at a temple of great stone blocks built against a cliff face. Behind him rushed a wide river. A road of weathered bricks led from the river to the temple.

Moving toward the temple, Bren hesitated at the sight of a statue that he guessed stood more than sixty feet tall. It was of a powerfully built man with the head of a crocodile.

Ugly, Bren thought. But different people had different tastes. He went on past it to the open doors of the temple. Inside was a large courtyard, where men and women walked serenely. Another large statue stood in the courtyard, this time that of a rearing crocodile set in a shallow pool.

The men, Bren saw, were all bare-chested and bald, and each wore a plain white kilt, while the women had short, dark hair and wore plain white gowns. As they noticed Bren, they all stopped dead, one after another, staring at him in surprise.

Then one of the watchers realized that Bren was armed. "He wears a sword!" the man shouted.

Suddenly the others were shouting at him.

"No weapons in our temple!"

"You blaspheme!"

"We are being invaded!"

This can't be right! These can't be the people the gnome mentioned. Did he trick me? Or did I hit the wrong icon on the amulet?

It didn't matter. In heartbeats he was encircled.

Bren decided to make a break for it. Turn *to page* 25.

Bren decided to brave out the situation. *Turn to page* 119.

Bren was curious about that mysterious pentagram. But the more he thought about it, the more he didn't want to trust his quest on entering a magical circle that wasn't directly related to his father's recovery.

Bren said to the monk, "That long-ago painter of my picture must have known I'd come here to give a warning to protect everyone here. Don't let anyone go near that pentagram. I don't know who put it here, or why. But I do know that it's too dangerous to be explored. I suspect it's a trap intended to destroy the temple."

"Thank you for the warning. It must, indeed, be why you were sent here."

"Uh, yes, of course. Just wall up the chamber and don't let anyone enter it again."

He took one last look at the pentagram. Behind him, Bren sensed the monk moving forward.

Bren turned quickly to see what was happening. *Turn to page 117.*

Bren suspected a trick and drew his sword. *Turn to page 26.*

As Bren pressed an icon on the amulet, something hit Bren's back with a slap. Even as the scene changed around him, he felt pain burning through him. It felt like hundreds of knife blades ripping at his back.

Suddenly a cold white light shone out of the darkness. A huge throne appeared. On the throne was ... he wasn't sure what it was, only that it had burning red eyes.

"You died again!" a cold, amused voice said. "You're dead now and you don't even know it."

"I, Darmu, cursed you and your father for all eternity. You allowed my spirit jar to be stolen again. I grow tired of humanity's carelessness with my soul. You will now walk the many paths of reality. Go, and never come here again."

Bren's spirit moved out of the darkness. He could see many halls and he started with the first one, walking down to its end, where he saw a version of himself dying as he was eaten by a crocodile.

His spirit form appeared at the beginning of the tunnels again. Bren could see millions of these tunnels with no end in sight. And he was going to be walking down them all. Forever.

The End

Without warning, Bren hurled his dagger straight at the target of those two red eyes. But something that might have been a furred and taloned hand snatched the dagger before it could strike home.

"My, what a pretty blade!" Darmu mocked. "And kind of you to give me such a present. But of course I couldn't think of keeping it. Here."

The dagger came hurtling back at Bren. He threw himself to one side, but the dagger followed him. He ducked, and it whizzed over his head, clipping off a lock of his hair—then turned and came after him. Bren had no shield, no way to catch it, not at the speed at which it was moving. All he could do was dodge and keep dodging.

But then Bren stumbled and fell. Before he could recover, the dagger neatly cut his throat.

As Bren choked on his own blood and his spirit rose from his body, he heard Darmu say, "Clever little thing. You shall make a fine slave. For all Eternity."

The End

"And so," Bren told the eerie pair, "the wizard wanted to use me as his tool to do what he couldn't. He wanted me to kill you or break your cauldron."

He watched their coldly smiling faces begin to frown.

"Ah me," the first one sighed. "What a shame. This lad has done us a service. He has put us in his debt."

"Yes," the second one agreed. "Normally, human, we would have feasted on you. Now, because of the debt, we cannot do that."

"We could send him back to kill the wizard," the first suggested.

"Ah, no, sister," the second one retorted, "I want to do that myself."

"If we send him on his way, the wizard destroys him."

Bren interrupted. "Excuse me, ladies, but I ... have an amulet." He showed it to them, warily keeping out of snatching distance. "If you could distract the wizard so that he can't keep watching me, I can get away from here. Then your debt to me would be repaid."

The two beings looked at each other. "We can do that," one said.

"The debt is paid," said the other. "Do not linger, human. We are growing very ... hungry."

Seeing their eyes beginning to glow with a new light, Bren hastily pressed an icon on the amulet.

Bren decided to return to the gnomish library and try again. *Turn to page 53.*

Bren wanted to try something new. *Turn to page 109.*

Bren looked around the deadly chamber, thinking that the wizard certainly came down here. Therefore, there had to be a way to get in without ...

Wait a minute. Slime *and* mold *and* fungi *and* tentacles? Wasn't that a little too much? Mold, maybe. Fungi, maybe. Even tentacles, maybe. But all that together in one place at the same time?

Then the silliness of the chamber struck him. *Illusion*, Bren thought. *It just has to be illusion*. He didn't know much about the nature of wizards, but he'd heard they had really strange senses of humor.

All right, then. He'd call it illusion, and not let himself think that if he was wrong, it might be a fatal mistake. It was illusion.

Bren walked out into the mold and fungi, choosing not to believe any of it was there—and all at once, it wasn't. He picked up the Tomtek jar, then shook his head. All that, and there was no telltale glyph on this one, either. With a sigh, Bren activated the next button on the amulet.

Turn to page 68.

Bren was getting pretty frustrated. There must be a way to get under Amela's guard. He faked a lunge to the right, trying to get her to follow, but she didn't fall for it. Before Bren could recover his balance, she stabbed him neatly and professionally in the sword arm.

His sword clattered from his hand. As Bren grabbed for his dagger, Amela, in a quick blur of movement, tossed her sword up, caught it by the blade, and bashed him over the head with the hilt. As consciousness fled, Bren heard her mutter, "Kid should bring a good price on the slave market."

She was right. He did. Bren was bought very quickly, and taken to a land far to the south. There he was bought again, this time by a merchant who was looking for a slave who was able to do his accounts.

For the rest of his life, Bren did the accounting for someone else. He never escaped. And he never did find out what happened to his father.

THE END

76

"There's no need for violence," Bren said in a merchant's smooth voice. "I am not your enemy. In fact, I think I'm very interested in what you're doing."

"Are you?" Morden asked sarcastically. "Are you really? Then come with us."

With the sorcerer behind him, Bren didn't really have a choice. Morden pressed a panel on the side of one bookcase, and it swung open. Beyond lay a spiral staircase leading down into darkness. Bren's hand went to the hilt of his sword—or rather, where the hilt of his sword should be.

The Sorcerer of Dex chuckled. "You didn't think I'd let you keep that weapon, did you?"

But he missed the dagger, Bren thought. *At least I still have that.*

The staircase took them down and down to a shadowy cavern under the house. Ahead was only one object, a large stone cut into the rough shape of a square. At first Bren thought it had been painted red. Then he realized, as the stench caught him, that it had been stained and restained with blood.

"The altar to Darmu," Morden said. "You are fortunate, little nuisance. You are going to get to meet Darmu personally."

Turn to page 98.

Without warning, Bren came out into a huge inner chamber. This had to be the heart of the tent, the place where the wolf priests brought their followers for whatever services they practiced.

In the center of the tent-room stood a white altar, its only ornament the image of a howling wolf's head done in what Bren's nose told him was fresh blood. On the altar was a Tomtek jar! It had a wolf head on its lid, and the head had a chipped ear. He recognized it!

Bren glanced quickly around, but saw no one. He hurried forward, holding his breath, snatched up the jar and ran with all his might, slashing his way through the walls of fabric with his sword. Behind him, he could hear men shouting and wolves howling. Bren ran with all his might, out into the clean night air.

He wasn't going to be able to keep up this pace much longer. The wolves were gaining! But now the city gates were near. Bren managed to gasp out his name and his father's name to the guards, and they let him into Dragon City and slammed shut the gates. Behind him, he heard frustrated howls.

When Bren had his breath back, he hurried home. But when he placed the jar on its shelf, there was no change in his father. There were no glyphs, either.

Bren's despair changed to hope when he realized he had also snatched up what looked like a strange amulet. It showed a red pentagram surrounded by six wolves.

As Bren held it, the pentagram and wolf icons began to glow. Suddenly he realized the truth of it: This was no mere amulet. This was a magical transporting device, and the small images and the center pentagram were the keys to making it work. Had the wolf priests used it to transport his father's jars? The only way to find out was to use it. But how? Should he start small and press the smallest icon? Or should he go straight for the pentagram?

Bren pressed the smallest wolf icon. *Go to 100.*

Bren pressed the pentagram. *Turn to page 106.*

Bren shot for the river's edge, but now there were other crocs between him and the river's edge. One of the smallest, barely his size, snapped at him, and Bren slashed out with his dagger, catching the crocodile in the belly. Blood filled the water.

As the monster crocodile came in, Bren swung the still jerking smaller crocodile into the monster's mouth. The great fangs snapped shut, and the monster dove with its unexpected cannibalistic meal. The other crocodiles followed, excited by the bloodshed. Bren swam frantically for shore and scrambled up onto dry land.

Judging from the grim expressions, no one was happy to see him. "There!" Bren shouted at all of them in glee, holding out the sacred stone. "I've survived your trial. You'll be happy to know that your Minion of Darmu is having a satisfactory meal—one that isn't me. Now keep your word and send me home!"

The last was said in challenge. Bren really doubted that they would keep their word, but he was too tired to run.

Then a ... force erupted around him.

Turn to page 10.

Bren didn't waste time. He turned and dashed off into the darkness, hoping that if he couldn't see anyone, they wouldn't be able to see him, either.

But how was he going to get out of here? He'd gotten in here, so there had to be at least the same way out. Where was it?

Then his foot struck something ... a step. The first step of a staircase. All right, he'd head up, and hope it led back to daylight.

But it didn't. At the top of the staircase, Bren found just more darkness.

And two red, glowing eyes.

"Did you enjoy your little romp all around my realm and back to me?" Darmu asked. "Do try it again. I really enjoy seeing you trying your best to hope, and then losing that hope. In fact," the demonic being added with a laugh, "I think you will be repeating this hope-then-hopelessness for a long time. For eternity, in fact."

The End

Bren felt a moment of dizziness. As he recovered he heard the unmistakable sound of a sword being drawn from its sheath.

"How, by the nine gods, did you get in here?"

It was a woman's voice. Bren blinked to clear his vision, then blinked again, this time in surprise. The woman was tall and beautiful in a stern, strong, no non-sense sort of way. She held her sword with confidence.

Bren dropped his hand to his sword's hilt but didn't draw it. "I didn't come here to fight," he told her. "I am Bren of House Tawilden of Dragon City. Those Tomtek jars at your feet are most likely my father's. If there's one with a glyph carved on its base, I really need it, and I'm not leaving without it."

"Back up out of lunging distance," she commanded. Then, with a shrug, the woman continued, "My name is Amela. I'm a mercenary, but there hasn't been too much work for a warrior."

"Then how did you get those jars?" Bren asked. "Did you turn thief?"

"Hardly. I ran into some very disagreeable priests who didn't think a woman should carry a sword." She grinned. "Let's just say that they learned better. And I took the jars they had been carrying, since the things looked valuable."

"All right," Bren said, "I can believe that. But I do need that jar, if it's here."

"Sorry, boy, I don't give up good loot just because you say it's yours."

Fighting to keep calm, Bren said, "Look, let's just check for the glyph. If it's there, I told you, I'm taking that jar. I don't want to fight a lady, but I'll do what I must. If the jar's not here, we'll let the Law handle the rest."

That was the wrong thing to say. The woman's face hardened, and her hand tightened on the hilt of her sword. Clearly she had little love for the Law. "I'm no lady, boy. And I'll search for the glyph. Period."

Bren backed up several paces to show her no threat, only now noticing that they were in a plain bedroom with nothing more than a bed, a chair—and the jars. It was probably a room in an inn. He watched Amela lift and examine each jar in turn, looking more impatient with each one. At last she turned to him again, sword raised.

"No glyph, boy. And I'm afraid that spells bad news for you. You seem like a nice fellow. I'm not going to enjoy killing you, but you shouldn't have threatened to bring in the Law."

With that, she attacked. In only a few moments, Bren gave up any ideas of not fighting a lady. Amela was clearly out to kill him, and he realized that there was a big difference between being good with a sword, as he was, and being a professional, as she was. He couldn't do much more than defend himself, but at least she wasn't able to do more than cut him a few times.

Bren was determined to win. *Turn to page 76.*

Bren thought that there really wasn't any reason for either of them to die. *Turn to page 122.*

Bren's merchant father had warned him about the danger of greed. Bren tiptoed warily about, looking but not touching the gleaming mountains of treasure. He decided not to take anything.

Then he saw a lovely crystal statue of a tower, lying beside the main mound of gold. Bren looked at it a long time, trying to turn away, but finally couldn't resist picking it up. How beautiful it was, so perfectly carved in every detail that it looked real.

Bren gasped in utter disbelief. As he held up the small tower, he saw a full-sized version of the tower suddenly shimmer into reality, just outside the dragon's cavern.

This might be the Sorcerer of Dex's trick. Bren turned away from the tower. ***Turn to page 89.***

Overwhelmed by wonder and curiosity, Bren approached the tower. ***Turn to page 58.***

Bren left without an argument. He would go home, he decided, and see if he could do anything there to help his father.

But he'd forgotten about the wolf priests. They were still hunting for him for killing one of their own. Bren heard a howl, saw great gray forms appear out of the forest, and grabbed for the amulet. But in his haste, he dropped it. Before Bren could snatch it up again, the wolf pack was on him. He cried out in agony as they tore his flesh and broke his bone. And then he felt his spirit leave his body.

Turn to page 38.

Bren went limp in the guard's grip. In the instant that the grip loosened, he twisted free and leaped out the window, down to the street that wasn't too far below. Behind him, as he began his run, he could hear shouting:

"Alarm! Thieves!"

Bren raced on into the night, hearing the commotion behind him grow louder as more and more people gathered around the shouting servants.

He'd heard such things happening in his neighborhood. First the people would come out of their homes to see what the noise was about. Then, soon after, the night watch would come at the call. There were bands of night watch guards all over the city, roaming and protecting those with business in the night.

Briefly he thought of finding some night watchmen and explaining what he had done. Then he rejected the thought. They'd never believe him. He'd broken into someone else's property, after all. He could only run.

Suddenly a hand shot out, pulled him into an alley, and threw him against the wall before he could draw his sword or even his dagger. A lean man in ragged clothes grinned at him. "Got the night watch after you, eh? You a thief or a killer?"

"Neither. I broke into a house, but—"

"Thief." The man shrugged. "Figured. You don't have the murderer look to you. Watch won't bother asking, though. They'll want you dead. Lighten their paperwork. Come on, kid, we're thieves. Let's get out of here."

Bren hesitated, glancing back at the shouting. And as soon as his back was turned, the man stabbed him. White-hot pain shot through him and, gasping for breath that wouldn't come, Bren crumpled. The last words he heard were the man yelling to the night watch:

"Here he is! Over here! Pulled a knife on me—I had to stab him. Just give me my thief-taking reward."

Bren tried to argue, but all that came out of his mouth was a rush of blood. And then there was nothing.

Turn to page 38.

Bren jumped up to catch the giant robin. His arms closed about the bird's legs, and for a few startling moments they were both flying. But a human was too heavy for even a giant bird to carry, and they both came tumbling down to the grass.

"Let me go!" the robin shrieked.

"Not till you tell me what I need to know."

"I don't know anything else. Help! Help! A human has me! Birds of the air, help!"

A second giant robin came flapping down and began fiercely pecking at Bren.

"Ow!" Bren yelled. "Stop that!"

But two giant sparrows soared down, and they, too, started pecking at Bren. Every peck hurt like the stab of a knife. Bren ducked his head to protect his eyes. But more birds were coming, and at last he lost his hold on the robin.

Now all the birds were pecking at him, stab, stab, stab. Bren struggled to defend himself, to draw his sword or dagger. But there were too many birds. Stab, stab, stab.

At last he could no longer feel the pain.

He could feel nothing.

THE END

Bren looked around in alarm. He was back in the wizard's workroom! This time, though, the wizard didn't seem to sense his sudden arrival. Very well, he'd get this over with here and now.

Bren lunged at the back of the wizard. But suddenly a white glow surrounded the wizard, and the second Bren's sword touched the white glow, his body froze in place.

The wizard chuckled. "Maybe you should have tried your dagger. Too late now. Since you insisted on returning here, you will now be helping me."

Bren could feel sweat pouring down his face. Nothing he could do would make even a finger twitch.

The wizard slapped his face, not very hard but hard enough to smart. "Pay attention, boy. It's just as easy for me to turn you into a frog as it is for me to give you a little assignment that will allow you to live, and in your rightful shape."

"I have a double problem, boy, and now it is your problem. There are two, well, let us call them … witches, yes, there's a nice, innocuous term for them. Witches." He chuckled as if at some private joke. "The two weird sisters can be found in the forest seven or so miles to the south of here. Since you seem to be in a killing mood, I want you to go and kill those two for me. Or, since I can see in your mind that you really don't like killing, you can crack their cauldron. One good smash with a hammer, or whatever is heavy that comes to hand, should do it. And that will break their power."

Even in Bren's desperate situation, he couldn't help wondering why a wizard with such great power couldn't solve this problem himself.

Clearly able to read Bren's thoughts, the wizard answered him. "I could go on for some time about the different vibrations and variant dimensional issues, all of which would mean nothing to you, you ignorant boy. So I'll simply say that what they are now makes them invulnerable to magic. They're not invulnerable to a blade, however. I'm no swordsman. But when a determined boy like yourself comes along, who am I to look a gift griffon in the beak? So, go kill them for me, or at least break that cauldron. I don't care which you do."

He snapped his fingers and the boy was free.

Bren fell to his knees, his entire body aching from having been held completely motionless. "Let me guess. I don't have a choice, do I?"

"Of course you do. You can live, or you can die. All right," the wizard added briskly, "I've explained things, given you a plan of action, and now it's time for you to act. If you try to run, trust me, boy, you'll truly regret it. And you'll never get to rescue your father. Good-bye."

Once again, the wizard turned his back on Bren. A door opened on the other side of the chamber.

Bren had no intention of doing the wizard's bidding. *Turn to page 52.*

Bren didn't feel he had any choice in the matter. The wizard was just too powerful. *Turn to page 111.*

Bren decided to take as much as he could before the dragon woke up. With his pack open, he started loading the five pockets with large gems and dazzling pieces of jewelry.

Soon his pouches were filled with the best in bracelets, fancy rings, and all sorts of gems that looked amazing. But there was so much more! Maybe he could fit in a few more gems ... yes, and maybe that gorgeous golden necklace.

He should leave. He had enough. But it seemed a shame not to take that pearl-encrusted scepter as well, yes, and that golden crown with the rubies—

When Bren pulled the crown free, a jangling waterfall of coins came with it. The dragon grunted, and Bren froze in fear. Was it waking up?

No. With a great effort, the dragon turned over in his sleep. The movement started an avalanche of golden treasures. And before Bren—weighted down with his loot—could move, he was crushed to death beneath it.

THE END

Bren ran down the mine shaft. But it dove deeper and deeper into the ground, and many corridors branched off on either side. Bren tracked his progress, but after a long time walking there was still not hint of an exit.

Then he saw it. There was a Tomtek jar lying on the ground. He lifted it, looking it over. No glyph. He wasn't sure it had been part of his father's collection, either. He put the jar back and continued walking.

As he walked, he kept hearing a low rumble. From time to time, dust fell from the ceiling. Once the walls shook, but he was not concerned

Then he went around a bend in the tunnel and found an amazing amount of jars just lying there. He gasped in pleasure. Oh look, look! This had to be his father's whole collection! Happily, he lifted the first one.

Then the cavern's tons of rock collapsed on him, killing Bren instantly.

A moment later, a glowing sprite returned to the wizard. "Ah well done," the wizard said. "You did make sure the illusions you cast made the poor young fool happy when he died?"

The light bobbed up and down.

"Then all's well that ends well."

The End

"Oh, no, please, no!" wailed a female voice from above. "Not again, not again!"

Bren heard the sound of small feet running down the stairs. In seconds a very pretty girl in a white silk dress, her long golden hair flowing out behind her, came hurrying down the stairs. She stopped short in front of Bren, searching his face with big, frightened blue eyes. "The tower—" she gasped. "Do you have the tower?"

"Slow down," Bren said. "First of all, my name is Bren. You are..?"

"I am called Orandell. But my name doesn't matter, not right now. Please tell me you have the crystal tower on you somewhere!"

Bren searched. He still had the crystal tower, but some odd inner warning told him not to mention it. Instead, he asked, "What are you talking about?"

"I wasn't always here," she cried. "No, no, I was once a princess in a magical kingdom, and I was free to do what I wished and go where I wanted. It was wonderful! Then—then an evil spell enclosed me in this tower. I don't even know how long I've been trapped in here. I just know that I can't get out. I'm never going to see my land again."

"And the little crystal tower?"

"The crystal tower is a very powerful magic object. It created and keeps real the tower we are in now. But unless you hold the tower when you come in here, the door disappears. Since you didn't take the crystal into the tower with you, there—there is no way to get out." Tears streamed down her pretty face. "You don't age in here. You can't kill yourself in here. You'll be trapped here forever."

She was so pretty and so unhappy that he couldn't bear it. "Don't cry," Bren said. "Please don't cry. We'll find a way out of here."

"There is none!" she wailed.

He ached to take her in his arms and comfort her, but didn't quite have the nerve. "It can't be as bad as all that."

"Can't it?"

Suddenly the sweet voice didn't sound sweet at all. The pretty girl and the charming tower blurred and changed.

And all at once Bren found himself not in a pretty tower but in a great, dark chamber. Confronting him wasn't the lovely young Princess Orandell—but the Sorcerer of Dex, black robes swirling about him.

"Did you think this was all going to end so prettily, hero boy?" the sorcerer asked with a thin smile. "Sorry to disappoint you. My master and I have other plans."

"Your ... master?"

"Why, Darmu, of course—who you will meet now."

Bren drew back in horror.

Bren thought he could attack before the wizard could get off a spell. *Turn to page 17*.

Bren decided to use the crystal tower to get out of there. *Turn to 108*.

Bren didn't really want to meet Darmu, but he thought that maybe a meeting would solve the mystery of the Tomtek jars. *Turn to page 98*.

Most houses of the sort Achernso owned had walled gardens at the back, and a quick check confirmed it.

In back of the house, Bren saw several trees growing near the wall. Climbing one only took a few heartbeats. The top of the wall was lined with shards of broken glass to keep off thieves, but Bren managed to vault safely over the glass and landed on his feet in the garden almost soundlessly. There didn't seem to be any guards around. Still, Bren kept to the shadows as much as possible.

The house, too, was dark, but Bren, peering through a narrow window, was sure he saw the familiar white shape of a Tomtek jar. He tried the door handle.

Look at this! Achernso doesn't lock his garden door.

Bren slipped into the house. Yes, those were definitely Tomtek jars—but which ones belonged to his father?

There was only one way to find out. Starting at the bottom of the many shelves, he upturned each jar in turn, looking for a glyph. Sorting out which jars belonged to his father could come later, after the man was healed.

He went through the eight jars on the lowest shelf and found nothing. He started on the next shelf up ... Bren sighed silently. He could swear this one with the dragon head belonged to his father, but there was no way to prove it. And it had no glyph. Nor did any others.

Suddenly he heard voices arguing in the hallway outside the room. Bren hesitated, ready to run out into the garden, but curious.

"I don't care what that old camel wants," one voice said, "I don't want to guard his stupid jars all night."

"He gave the orders, and he pays the bills," the other voice answered. "Remember, I relieve you at sunrise."

"Got it. See you later."

A thin sliver of light from a lantern slid under the door. Uh-oh. The guard was just outside the room—and now Bren heard a hand turning the door's handle.

He could try to knock out a guard. *Turn to page 65.*

Or maybe he should just run for it. *Turn to page 103.*

There didn't seem to be any other choice. Holding his breath, Bren rushed into the chamber. His hands closed around the Tomtek jar—but his feet slipped on the slimy floor. Bren fell flat. Before he could get his hand on the amulet, a tentacle squirmed out from the wall and closed about his wrist. Two more closed about his body. Bren struggled wildly, trying to get his sword or dagger out.

Then a third tentacle wrapped itself around his face. Now Bren fought just to get a breath. But there was no air, only slime, slime filling his nose, his mouth, his eyes. With his last desperate gasp, Bren knew he had failed.

The tentacles opened fang-lined maws and settled down on their nice, fresh prey to feed.

THE END

Jogging quickly north in his new armor, Bren felt amazing. He had a new spring to his step and his confidence had gone way up. He knew he could find all the rest of the jars, including the one with the glyph and get them back in time, he just knew it.

Zzzzzzt!

What was that? It had been the oddest swooshing sound in the air. Then a large crash sounded off to Bren's left as whatever it had been hit the ground. The palm trees of the beach blocked his view of what it was.

Bren briefly thought of investigating. He found himself spoiling for a fight for some reason. But the thought of his father dying in his bed changed his mind and spurred Bren on. He started running and was amazed at the speed he could reach without being at all winded.

Zzzzzzzzt!

A hundred yards ahead of him a huge bronze javelin embedded itself in the ground, vibrating with the force with which it had been thrown.

Zzzz …

Bren's body was pinned to the ground by the javelin that had just been thrown by the bronze statue. Bren, or at least his spirit, found himself pumping a huge bellows by a giant's forge. The blacksmith god who had snared him smiled at him.

"Imagine thinking you could steal treasure from the storehouse of the gods. That armor was my work, little thing. Don't worry," the god added, "I'll remove the curse on your father, just to make you happier. It wouldn't do for you to not have your mind on my work."

THE END

"All right," Bren said with a bravery he didn't really feel, "let me see Darmu. We have a lot to discuss."

He was suddenly alone in utter darkness. Trying not to shiver, Bren drew his dagger and stood waiting, his heart pounding, for something to happen. Then two red fires appeared out of the blackness, and after a second, Bren realized that they were eyes. Demonic eyes.

As his own eyes began adjusting a little to the darkness, Bren thought he could see a ... shape, blacker even than the darkness, sitting on a huge stone throne.

"Ah, the little mortal fool dares to come before me," a chill, cruel, amused voice said. "Know that I am Darmu, fool, and tremble!"

"I'm not going to tremble," Bren said, pleased with how level his voice sounded. "You have already cursed my father and me. Since I don't have anything else to lose, I'll just say that I don't think what was done to us was just. We had no way of knowing your jar was among the collection. And if you're angry at anyone, it should be the wolf priests who were the thieves."

There was utter silence. Then Darmu ... laughed. It was a terrible sound, like the crashing of great boulders. "Justice? What has that concept to do with me?" For an instance, the dark shape on the throne looked almost like a wolf. Then it was a crocodile. Then it was ... a dark, nameless shape once more. "If fools wish to worship me, that is their problem. I am no god, I am a demon! And I do what pleases me!"

"But you couldn't stop the wolf priests from stealing the jars," Bren retorted.

"I had no wish to stop them."

This didn't make sense. "But—but if you wanted the jars stolen," Bren asked, "why were we cursed?"

The dark shape stirred impatiently. "Enough. Come, little mortal, entertain me, and you may yet live."

At a sharp command from Darmu, a figure stole out from the shadows. It held a sword and had the body of a sleek, powerful warrior—but it also had the head of a snarling leopard.

Bren no longer had his sword, but he would fight with his dagger. *Turn to page 115.*

Bren thought he'd better try to get out of here. He had the amulet, after all. *Turn to page 53.*

Bren thought he'd better try to get out of here without the amulet. *Turn to page 80.*

Bren decided to make a deal with Darmu first. *Turn to page 35.*

There was a dazzling flash of light, and suddenly Bren found himself in darkness. Hot, smelly darkness. It stank of blood and ... was that brimstone?

Yes, it was, he realized. Now that his vision had cleared, Bren saw that he stood in a vast volcanic cave. Lava pools glowed and bubbled wherever the cavern's jagged black floor was broken, making the cave searingly hot.

Then a horrible roar echoed throughout the cave. Two huge, hideous creatures were fighting each other. Bren didn't know what they were. One looked like some sort of lizard beast, but one with many heads. If one head was destroyed, two more sprang up.

But the other monster was worse. This creature was the stuff of nightmare. It was mostly a huge blob of sickly pink flesh. Embedded in the flesh were many different sets of fanged jaws. Its body also had horns and oddly shaped eyes, and then Bren saw why.

The monster had just enveloped three of the lizards' heads, and right before Bren's eyes, the flesh of the monster changed and new, lizard-like eyes and jaws appeared in three different places on the blob monster. The creature was slowly moving toward the lizard and its flesh was covering the lizard. It looked as though no matter how many new heads sprang up from the body of the lizard, eventually it would be absorbed.

Then Bren saw the unmistakable shape of a Tomtek jar right in the center of the blobby mass.

"Ahem, how do you like my pet?" a deep voice asked.

Bren turned, and his heart skipped a beat. The being who'd just spoken was a blue dragon, a huge, presumably immensely powerful one. It was old, the blue faded along the edges of the scales, but there was nothing slow in the way it rose to loom over him, standing between him and the passage that seemed the only way out.

Trying to sound more bold than he felt, Bren retorted, "I like everything but the Tomtek jar in its belly. That's my father's jar and I've come to take it back."

"Really?" the dragon asked, a world of skepticism in it voice. "That's interesting, but hardly important. At least not to me. My name is Garyant. I would know your name before I eat you."

"I'll prove a nasty tasting tidbit and I expect to give you a bellyache for quite a white," Bren replied.

"Ah, ah, you're a brave little thing aren't you? What is your name if you would?" asked the dragon a second time.

It moved a step towards him, and its tongue licked hungrily over its long, sharp fangs. Bren had to do something if he didn't want to be the dragon's dinner.

Bren thought there was no choice but to fight the dragon. *Turn to page 20.*

Bren decided his best chance was to bargain with the dragon. *Turn to page 42.*

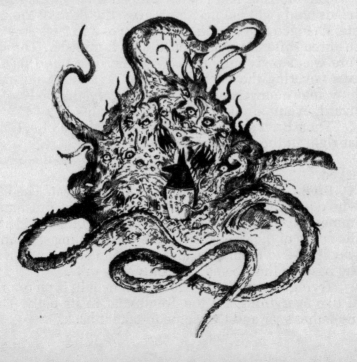

Bren drew his sword and charged the wizard.

The wizard still didn't turn around. He simply reached over his shoulder and said something that made fire tingle up and down Bren's body. The sword fell from his hand. He dropped to his hands and knees with a cry of pain. But the cry came out sounding like the yelp of a wolf. Bren writhed, feeling muscles straining and bones changing. Hair sprang out all over his body. His face grew long and his teeth grew sharp.

Bren had become a wolf. In an instant, he forgot all about the Tomtek jars. He forgot all about his father. He forgot he'd ever been human, and bounded off to find the rest of his wolf pack.

THE END

Getting out of here in a hurry seemed like a good idea. The jar with the glyph didn't seem to be here, and he could always get the Dragon City Law after Achernso to retrieve the other stolen jars after his father was healed. Bren climbed the garden wall again, once more avoiding the danger of the glass-studded wall top, and ran into the night.

It was time for him to investigate the wolf priests.
Turn to page 63.

Bren didn't dare ask the villagers any questions about a possible dragon sleeping under their waterfall. He didn't want the Sorcerer of Dex to learn what he was doing. That meant that Bren had to go see the cave for himself.

Leaving the village behind, Bren headed towards the waterfall. He started climbing the rocks until he was behind the waterfall and found himself in a huge cavern.

A handful of gold pieces lay at his feet. There was a strange smell of snake and smoke coming from within the cavern. It was true, then, Bren thought. Evidently, dragons liked to make their homes behind waterfalls when they had the chance.

The cave was uncomfortably warm, and as Bren warily moved in deeper, he could see the reason for the heat. The dragon was in its lair, snoring away on top of a massive mountain of treasure. It was another red one, though more orange than true red, and each of its scales was taller than a man. Its body twisted in and out of the treasure pile, and in its sleep it snorted sparks and smoke that raised the temperature of the cave to "uncomfortable for humans" levels.

Amazed at the wealth displayed here, Bren had to fight to keep himself from diving in and loading himself down with gold and gems. He warily tiptoed around the treasure pile and noted several other cave tunnels going off in many different directions. There were glints of light from some of them.

The dragon stirred in its sleep, and the movement sent tons of treasure shifting and slithering down into the cavern. Bren had to scramble for his very life as a wave of gold in the form of coins and chalices and treasure-filled coffers slid down the treasure mountain and spread out over the cavern's floor.

Several gems with their own inner glows had been revealed. In all the legends Bren had ever read, such glowing gems meant great magical power. It could be well worth the danger to climb the pile and take them.

Wait a minute, what was that? A crystal staff with a glowing green human skull at the top—that was a wishing staff! The mayor of Dragon City used one to ward off evil, since every year the staff glowed with the power of a magical wish. That wish was traditionally always used to help the city prosper.

But this staff, Bren thought, reading the glyphs on it, only held one wish. Bren picked up the glowing staff, knowing that there was a wish in it he could use. Holding the staff in both hands he said, "I wish my father had never collected the Tomtek jar that led to our curse."

The staff glowed bright for an eye-blink and then went dark. Bren didn't know if the wish had worked or not, but he liked to think it did.

"If my wish saved my father and my family," Bren said, "it was worth losing this wonderful bit of magic."

Bren tossed the now-useless staff back on the pile. Now what should he do? Should he take some treasure, or should he explore the other caverns?

Bren didn't want to risk taking things from under the body of the sleeping dragon. He decided to see what was in the side caverns. *Turn to page 55.*

Bren couldn't leave without taking a closer look at the treasure. *Turn to page 33.*

"And who would you be?" came a cold voice from the other side of the chamber Bren now found himself in.

This was a room with a jumble of tables and shelves filled with, well, he didn't know what half those things were, except that they smelled like a combination of cinnamon and something foul. Those didn't matter, though, because a wizard stood on the other side of the room.

Wizards weren't always easy to spot since they usually looked just like anyone else—unless, of course, they were wearing their ceremonial robes, but this wizard would stand out in any crowd, since he was radiating an aura of blue light.

"I didn't invite you here," he said to Bren, "and I see you have the amulet of the wolf priest on your person. The only way you could have gotten that amulet—an amulet I made, by the way—is by killing one or two of those foolish priests and taking it from their altar. Suddenly I think I really don't like you." His hands began to glow with fire at his fingertips.

"I mean you no harm," Bren said hastily. "And I didn't mean to trespass. My father lies dying in our home. Those priests stole our Tomtek jars. All I'm trying to do is get those jars back to heal my father and remove a terrible curse from our family."

"I care nothing for your problems," the wizard growled. "You can leave my tower, without that amulet. I'll let you live to fight another day. We're several days walk from your town. Just head south and bother me no more."

Bren figured that he'd better go while he could. *Turn to page 84.*

Bren wanted to find out what the wizard knew about the Tomtek jars. *Turn to page 66.*

"The heart is yours," Bren said quickly. "You earned it through conquest."

The wolf snarled. "Flatterer! I hate flattery! You didn't think about the riddle at all, just said what you thought I would like to hear." The wolf got to its feet, its massive gray body towering over Bren. "That was a bad mistake."

Bren backed away, drawing his sword. "I didn't mean to insult you."

The wolf gave its growling laugh. "And do you think that tiny thorn will slay me?"

Bren thought quickly. "It will if you swallow me," he said. "It'll go with me, and lodge its point somewhere inside your gut. It'll start wearing away a tiny hole in there. You'll die slowly from it."

"Bah! You're more trouble than your bad-tasting flesh is worth," the wolf snapped. "Begone!"

Turn to page 44.

Bren didn't want to come up against either Darmu or the Sorcerer of Dex. He held up the crystal tower, and sure enough, a door opened in the real tower's smooth wall. Bren raced through it, and then threw the crystal tower down as hard as he could and stomped on it for good measure. The crystal tower shattered—and the real tower instantly disappeared.

He was safe, at least for now. But Bren knew that now he had to warn Dragon City that the Sorcerer of Dex was alive. It was a long way back to the city, but he finally made it.

But when Bren tried to tell everyone what he'd seen, no one took him seriously. It was too fantastic a story. At last Bren gave up all hope of warning anyone at all. By that time, he'd lost track of the days. It was far too late to save his father.

When the Sorcerer of Dex did attack, no one in Dragon City was ready. Including Bren. When the city fell, everyone, including Bren, died with it.

THE END

Bren found himself in sunshine, in a lovely green valley. Where was he? Could this be ...

Yes. This must be the far end of Dragon Valley, many long days' travel from Dragon City. He'd never been this way with his father, but the man had described that ancient carving of a dragon's head up near the waterfall Bren saw now. It was said to be nearly a twin of the one carved near Dragon City's own waterfall, and had probably been carved by the same ancient people.

Why had he appeared here, though?

He could only move on. Bren started walking toward the mountain village near the end of the valley.

It was a long walk. Luckily for him the apple trees and plum trees he saw along the way were in fruit, and the river was clean enough to drink. After two days of hard trudging, Bren stood in front of the large gates, looking on in wonder. Whoever had built Dragon City's gates must have been the same man to design these, too.

"Pretty impressive aren't they?" a guard said. The man was leaning against a tall spear. He was dressed in drab clothes with an oversized helmet.

Pretty silly for a village this size, Bren thought but politely didn't say.

"A Wizard made it in the blink of an eye, last week," the guard continued. "We don't even have enough men to work the gates properly; we just leave them open most of the time. I know everyone here—but I don't know you."

"I'm Bren of House Tawilden."

"Sorry, don't know that house." The guard must have been bored, because he added chattily, "You and your house coming to live here? If you are, you get over to the mayor's new office before all the good plots of land are gone. You need a place to stay, try the Red Dragon Inn. It's pretty comfortable, and my brother's the cook there."

"Well, thank you, I'll take both of those suggestions," Bren replied tactfully and entered the village.

The mayor's mansion was a big, sprawling building a good walk down the main road from the gate. It, too, seemed too big for a village this size, and it was a busy place, with several groups of men deep in conversation. But then Bren's attention was caught by the sight of an impressive man dressed all in black.

He blinked, looked again in sheer disbelief, trying not to stare. No, there was no mistaking that sharp profile, nor that star-shaped birthmark on the man's cheek. This was not a wizard, a magic-user who might be either evil or good, but a sorcerer, a worker of dark magic—and what was more, he was one every schoolchild of Dragon City knew: This was the Sorcerer of Dex. The man had been supremely evil and it had taken all the good magic-users to destroy him, wrecking most of the city in the process.

But everyone knew that magic-users were notoriously difficult to kill. It must have taken the sorcerer a long time to recover, but clearly he was back to himself. Just as clearly, the Sorcerer of Dex had given up on trying to take Dragon City again, at least for now. Was he going to try taking over this village instead, just as a place to start?

There was another possibility. At the Dragon City end of this long valley, that matching carving of a dragon head had commemorated the dragon that had slept deep underground. "The Treasure of the Red Dragon" was a famous legend of Dragon City. A forester was said to have discovered a cave behind the waterfall. In the cave was a massive treasure hoard with a gigantic red dragon sleeping in the middle of it. It wasn't until an invasion of savage green dragons attacked the city that the red dragon had awakened and taken to the skies to protect its lair—and incidentally had saved Dragon City.

Did that mean there might be a similar dragon asleep on a golden hoard under this waterfall as well? If so, that treasure might be what had brought the sorcerer here.

Bren though that he needed to warn someone here about the sorcerer. *Turn to page 15.*

Bren though he'd better check and see if there really was a hidden treasure, and get to it before the sorcerer could. *Turn to page 104.*

Curses, wizards ... what's next? Bren thought, heading south through the forest. *No, maybe I shouldn't even ask that!*

The wizard hadn't been too clear on where he'd find the two witches, or whatever they were. The implication was, uneasy though that made Bren, that they would find him. But every time he thought of just getting out of here, he remembered how powerful that wizard was, and kept going. He didn't have a doubt that the wizard was watching him through magical means, or that the wizard would be well able to take a nasty revenge on him if he just fled.

It was getting pretty dark. Soon he would have to stop for the night. Bren was just starting to look for a place to camp till morning when a voice said softly, "Ah, look."

A second voice added, "Yes ... and he is so delightfully cursed."

Two figures slipped out of darkness. They were both female, both tall, one Bren's height, the other even taller, and both were so lean they looked almost like skeletons covered with dead-white skin. Both of the ... beings wore long black gowns and had narrow faces with dark eyes that glowed eerily in the dark.

"Welcome to our home," one said.

"Have you fed?" the second one asked. The way she asked the question made Bren very happy he hadn't taken a bite.

"I'm not really hungry, thank you," he said.

"We will be."

What were these creatures? The wizard had called them witches, but as though he hadn't wanted to tell Bren the truth. These were witches who had become ... what? Vampires? Ghouls? The Undead of some other equally dangerous sort?

And he wants me to kill them? Bren thought. *Maybe I'd better settle for smashing their cauldron.*

"You can see I'm cursed?" Bren asked, not knowing what else to say.

The one on the left purred, "Why of course."

The one on the right added, "It's a wondrous black mist surrounding your body. And it had to have been Darmu who laid it on you. He's such a jester, demon-god that he is."

Suddenly hopeful, Bren asked, "Could you remove the curse from me and my father?"

"We could," said one.

"For a price," added the other.

Now why do I suspect the price would be my blood? "The price?" Bren said with as much merchant charm as he could manage. "Shall we say a nice bit of information?"

The two beings looked at each other. "I doubt that any information a human might have would matter to us," said one.

"And why you would want to be rid of the intriguing darkness is a mystery," added the other.

"Shall we feed him first?"

"Oh yes. The human looks so weary."

Oh joy. "That really won't be necessary," Bren cut in.

"But we do have some excellent ... soup. And you are our guest, after all."

At her gesture (her fingernails, Bren noticed, were long, sharp and blood-red), a cauldron appeared.

Bren wasn't about to eat or drink with them. But he had to do something to get out of this.

Bren thought that he could smash the cauldron with a large rock to his left. *Turn to page 32.*

Bren didn't like the look of them, but these beings had so far done nothing to him. He decided to warn them of the wizard's intentions. *Turn to page 74.*

As they moved to the river, Bren couldn't find any way to avoid fighting Garlun-ta.

"Here is where you make your last sacrifice," the man said.

Bren began the stretching exercises he'd been taught by Sword Master Trign to loosen his muscles before a fight. But as he did, he looked over his opponent and didn't like what he saw. Garlun-ta was tall and muscular, clearly in the prime of life. He held a strange weapon, its hilt carved with green scales, its blade made up of razor-sharp pieces of green glass like large teeth. Catching Bren's glance, Garlun-ta said, "You will be facing the Weapon of Darmu. We use this for any sacrifice we give up to our god."

"You swear on the honor of your god that if I win I will take the jar and you will send me back to my home?" Bren asked.

Garlun-ta dipped his head to Bren. "In the unlikely event that you win this challenge, my people will abide by our agreement."

"Since I'm voluntarily giving myself up for this contest, shouldn't Darmu take the curse from my body and my father's body?" Bren said in an attempt to bargain a chance for his father even if he lost.

Garlun-ta laughed. "An excellent point. No sacrifice to Darmu should be cursed before it goes to serve Darmu." To the others, he commanded, "Bring the Bowl of Darmu."

The large, oval bowl was made of green jade. It rested on a large bronze stand.

"You will wash your face and hands in the bowl, thinking of your father all the while," Garlun-ta ordered. "The power of Darmu remove your curse and your father's in exchange for the sacrifice you are about to make."

Bren didn't see anything in the bowl, but when he put a tentative hand into it, he felt water, or what he hoped was only water. He washed his hands and face in the mystical water, and then glanced up—and froze in shock at what he saw.

"Yesss," Garlun-ta hissed, "you now see usss asss we truly are."

The only way Bren knew he still faced Garlun-ta was by the tattoos on the scaly body of the … thing. All the others had changed as well, with scaly arms ending in talons and long jaws filled with fangs.

Resigned, Bren drew his sword and dagger. Would the weapons even cut the flesh of the monster he faced?

Monstrous roars of excitement filled the river valley as Garlun-ta rushed Bren. Bren hastily dodged, parried, dodged again. He saw his opening, and lunged with all his might. But the point of his sword bent double instead of driving even an inch into the leathery chest. Garlun-ta brought his weapon around in a huge swing, and Bren ducked frantically. Even so, the razor-sharp glass cut into his arm.

Biting back a cry of pain, Bren told himself, *Not that bad, it's not that bad.* He couldn't hold the sword level, though, and even if he could, where could he possibly strike on that scaly hide?

Not the hide! Bren tossed his dagger up into the air, caught the blade and in one smooth motion, threw it straight into Garlun-ta's eye and brain. The monster dropped to his knees, then fell flat.

The roars of the others stopped in that second as every one of them realized what the defeat of their leader meant: Darmu was not pleased with his worshipers.

Silently, they took Bren to the inner sanctum and handed him the spirit Tomtek jar. Then the magic of Darmu transported him back home.

Bren's father stirred, then woke with a start. "Bren! You're back!"

"The curse is gone, too!"

For the first time in a long time, Bren wasn't worried about his father. He had succeeded in his quest and even the gods must surely be satisfied with what he'd done.

The End

Bren knew his dagger was sharp enough to pierce anything. He moved into the fight. The leopard-man hissed at him, then lunged. Bren dodged, then whirled, stabbing up—

Missed. The leopard-man moved like the cat he half-was. Bren gasped as the sword cut him across his dagger arm. He hastily switched the knife to his sword hand, but now he felt awkward. It didn't help that the leopard-man was moving even more smoothly than before—or that he was so inhumanly quick. Bren tried cutting at him with the dagger as the leopard-man circled him, but missed completely.

The leopard-man made a sound that could have been a snarl or a laugh, and threw away his sword. He threw himself on Bren, one sharp-clawed hand catching Bren's wrist, blocking the dagger. Bren smelled the blood-reek of the creature's breath, caught a quick, terrible glimpse of long white fangs—

Then the leopard-man's fangs had closed on Bren's throat. He fought to get free, to get air … just one lungful of air …

His struggles weakened, then stopped. As his spirit left his suffocated body, Bren heard Darmu's chill laugh.

"Now, little fool, you will know the true curse. Now you will serve me as my slave for all eternity."

THE END

Bren drew his dagger, planning to dive under the crocodile and stab up into its belly. The crocodile, though, had plans of its own. Too late, Bren realized that Darmu must have given it unusual intelligence. It dove before he could, and his attempt to stab it managed only a shallow, harmless slash on its tough upper scales. The crocodile twisted about with frightening speed. Bren saw the great jaws open—and then the knife-sharp fangs snapped down on him. Struggling in vain to free himself, he screamed in agony, and that drove the last of the air from his lungs. There was nothing left to do now but ... drown.

The End

Bren nearly laughed out loud. All that movement by the monk had been nothing but a deep, ceremonial bow. Bren did his best to imitate it.

"Your words are wise," the monk said. "What you advise shall be done." He paused. "Do you wish to stay here?"

For a moment, Bren did want to stay in that nice, peaceful place. But he couldn't afford the time. "I would like to stay here," Bren replied, "but I'm afraid I can't take you up on the offer."

"Then do you wish guidance from here?"

"No thank you. That isn't necessary. I have my own way out of here."

With that, Bren pressed another icon on the amulet at random. *Turn to page 61.*

With that, Bren pressed the icon of a wolf with a forest behind it. *Turn to page 95.*

Bren whipped out his sword. "Sorry, gentlemen, but I'm afraid I can't stay." He started warily backing away.

The sorcerer laughed as if Bren had said something truly funny. "Oh, really?"

He gestured, and the sword was jerked from Bren's hand. It soared up to the ceiling, then turned, point down, and came hurtling straight at Bren. He grabbed a chair, lifting the heavy thing just in time. The sword buried itself in the chair, not his heart. Bren hurled the chair at the sorcerer—

But Morden brought a stone vase down on Bren's head with crushing force. Bren didn't even have time for a cry of pain. Light exploded behind his eyes.

Then there was darkness.

Turn to page 38.

A tall, burly man with crocodile tattoos all over his chest and arms, strode forward, and the crowd parted to let him through.

"What do you do here, barbarian?" he snapped at Bren.

"I'm on a quest," Bren said, trying to sound much braver than he felt just then. "My father is dying because wolf priests stole his Tomtek jars. We have been cursed by … by a god and must bring the jars home or die."

"What is that to do with us?"

"Have you recently acquired a Tomtek jar, maybe with a crocodile head on it?"

All the others gasped. The burly man glared at Bren. "I would know your name, young one, before we discuss the spirit of our god."

Bren hesitated. "Blade is my family name," he lied warily. "And you?"

"You may call me Garlun-ta, high celebrant of the great Darmu. You see his visage in the pool of our outer temple."

Wait a minute, Bren thought. *There's something weird here. If Darmu is the reason the wolf priests stole our jars, why does he look like a crocodile instead of a wolf? Or does he really look like something else entirely? Can that be true? If so, how many people is he tricking into worshipping him?*

"I sense our god's curse on you," Garlun-ta continued. "It lies over your body like a dark cloud. Just recently we did, indeed, gain a spirit jar, what you northerners call a Tomtek jar. It rests now in state in the inner temple. It was stolen from here hundreds of years ago. It is not leaving again."

Bren frowned. "I have to return one special jar to my home to save my father's life. I need only know if your jar has a glyph carved on it."

"We do not aid those who are cursed by Darmu. Go away, boy."

"No, I will not." Boldly, Bren added, "I didn't come all this way to be stopped by someone like you. If your god cursed me, it's because he wants me to recover the jar."

Would Garlun-ta believe that story? The man did stop cold for a moment, as if he wasn't used to anyone disagreeing with him. Then he snarled, "So be it, fool. You have a choice. In times past we have let a minion of Darmu decide things. You may dive into the river to retrieve a sacred stone. If you survive that choice, the stone's magic sends you home."

"And my second choice?"

"That choice is to fight me in a duel to the death. If you win, you will be given our spirit jar and magically transported back to your home." Garlun-ta added with a thin smile, "Of course you will not win such a battle. No one can, since I am the favored one of Darmu. Come, what is your choice?"

He wasn't getting anywhere with these people. Bren decided to go back to the gnomish library and try another way. *Turn to 7.*

Bren could swim pretty well. He chose the river challenge. *Turn to page 46.*

If the only way to get to the jar was to fight Garlun-ta, Bren thought, so be it. *Turn to page 113.*

Bren returned to the gnome's library.

The gnome gave a sign of relief. "There you are! I was hoping you'd be back. Alive, too."

"I pressed the wrong icon before."

"I thought you had. Visited the crocodile people, did you? My, you must have had a wild time! They don't like strangers."

"I noticed."

"Yes, yes, I'm amazed you survived. Now, press the right icon this time, lad, if you want to meet the ones who were here about the wolf priests."

Bren pressed the icon, wondering—and trying not to worry about—who he'd meet this time.

Turn to page 30.

Suddenly Bren had an idea. He took as big a leap backwards as he could manage to give himself some room, and then lowered his sword. "This is silly," he announced.

"Silly!" Amela echoed in surprise.

"That's what I said. Look, my father's a merchant, and not a poor one. You didn't steal the jars from him, you took them from the thieves. So my father and I have no real quarrel with you."

"Go on," Amela said warily.

"If you're really a mercenary, you fight for pay. And you'll get paid very well if you can keep your half of this deal."

She lowered her sword. "I'm listening."

Bren looked about for something to write on and with, and grabbed a piece of charcoal from the room's fireplace and tore off a piece of a sheet. Writing quickly, he said, "Instead of trying to find buyers for the jars, and maybe not finding any, take the lot to my father's house with this note and you'll get paid the amount listed. In exchange, I won't call in the Law. Oh, and we both get to live. Do we have a deal?"

She looked at the amount he'd written down, and smiled. "We have a deal. But why aren't you coming back with me?"

"I'd like to, but I have other places to go," Bren said with a weary grin, and pressed an icon on the amulet.

Turn to page 121.

Before Bren could knock, the doors opened sound-lessly. The temple chamber was huge, a long rectangle lit by row after row of candles. Hundreds of chanting monks in orange robes floated in the air, all of them pointing to an altar gleaming with gold, deep within the temple. More illusions? Was anyone here real?

Bren headed down the long corridor to the altar. A small boy in the same orange monkish robes stood before it. Bren stared. The surface of the altar was covered with Tomtek jars.

"Your coming was foretold," the boy said. "For a thousand years, we have had a choice and only you can help us to know which way to go."

"And the jars?"

"We shall have those belonging to your father returned to him after you make the choice."

Bren thought that most of his father's jars must be here. Surely returning all of these jars would cure his father of any curse. But … no glyphs were carved on any of them. Bren sighed. "Tell me more about the choice."

The monk bowed politely. "Please, follow me."

Bren was led down a long, smoothly-cut flight of black marble stairs. "This monastery has been in these mountains for a thousand years," said the young monk as they climbed down. "In the early days of the temple, when the caverns were being excavated below the tem-ple, an unexpected chamber was found. As our torches brought light into the darkness, we saw a strange penta-gram appear on the dark stone."

Bren frowned at the floor of the large chamber as the monk's torch illuminated a red glowing pentagram. It looked all too familiar. Bren sniffed the air, smelling blood again. Oh yes, he was looking at the pentagram of the wolf.

"That's fresh blood," he said.

"Indeed," the monk agreed. "There must be strong magic at work here, though one that is foreign to us. We do not believe in spilling blood. What is truly alarming is that the blood forming the pentagram always stays wet and can't be wiped away because it restores itself instantly. Over the centuries, any monks who have stepped onto this pentagram have vanished forever."

"But what has this to do with me?"

"Several centuries ago, one of our order had the gift of prophecy. He saw a traveler, a merchant, giving us information on this mystery. Look."

Bren looked at the indicated wall. There, weathered with time but still perfectly clear was a painting of ... Bren. That monk really must have had the gift of prophesy!

"What choice do you want me to make?" he asked.

"It is simple, and nothing that should, we trust, harm you. You can leave this chamber and completely ignore this pentagram. Or you can enter the pentagram. We know that if you do, the pentagram will disappear. No disgrace attaches to either choice."

Bren figured that if he went through the pentagram, he could always use the amulet if he got into trouble. *Turn to page 24.*

Going through the pentagram, Bren though, was just asking for more trouble. *Turn to page 71.*

The thick forest quickly gave way to high hills. Bren climbed till he saw the mouth of a huge cave, the home of the wolf spirit. To one side of the cave was a pile of skulls. Well, that wasn't too unusual a sight for a wolf's den, Bren guessed.

But at the top of the pile were two dragon skulls.

"What sort of wolf could have killed something as powerful as a dragon?" he wondered aloud.

"I think you'll find I'm more than enough to kill most things," a voice snarled from inside the cave. "Why are you here, little morsel?"

Bren suddenly saw two man-tall yellow eyes burning out of the darkness. "Are you the god the wolf priests of my land worship?"

"I'm worshipped," the wolf replied. "But I'm not a god. I'm a spirit. I think you don't know the difference, but I do and that's all that counts."

Bren didn't think it was wise to argue terms with anything big enough to kill a dragon. "My father lies dying because wolf priests stole Tomtek jars from my home and placed a curse on us both. I'm here to get that curse removed."

A wolf's head, shaggy, gray, and larger than Bren was tall, moved slowly out of the cave. "As you have stepped onto my lands, you and your father are no longer cursed. As I didn't tell my worshipers to steal your jars, you have no claim on me. Please help me, little morsel, in deciding why I shouldn't eat you."

Those fangs were longer than any sword, and those jaws were large enough to swallow him in one gulp. With desperate humor, Bren said, "We mortals are a bony lot. I have it on good authority that we taste terrible, too. It's possible you should reconsider gnashing me."

The wolf actually gave a growling chuckle. "True, true. I have eaten humans in the past and have not liked the taste of any of them. You do have courage, tiny morsel. What would you have me do?"

Bren hesitated, then said, "While my father is alive, which is what I wanted most, jars of great value have been taken by your people. But there is one in particular that I need. It is said to have a strange glyph carved onto it."

The wolf frowned, an alarming sight. "That I know nothing about. It sounds like the jar of Darmu, and I do nothing with that being."

"Darmu! Isn't he a wolf god?"

The wolf spirit snarled. "Never! That is a demon-god, not one of my kin! He deceives humans into worshiping him. Come, before I taste you, little morsel, what else do you want of me?"

Sometimes, Bren told himself, a merchant gambled all on the role of the dice. "I would get back the richest of the stolen jars with your help and thank you for your justice in the matter."

"Would you, indeed? I would ask you a riddle first, little morsel," the wolf retorted. "I am a hunter. My life depends on my skills in the chase. Say I take down a deer, after a long run where it almost escaped me several times. I rip into its chest and hold the dead creature's still warm heart in my jaws. Is that heart owned by the deer or is that heart, at the exact moment of me about to swallow it, owned by me?"

Bren thought about the riddle and he also thought about what type of creature asked that riddle.

Bren gave the answer he hoped the wolf would want to hear. *Turn to page 106.*

The answer seemed obvious: the deer. Bren answered right away. *Turn to page 49.*

Bren thought the riddle sounded suspiciously simple and needed more careful consideration. *Turn to page 29.*

Bren followed the spark of light down the stairs. The chamber at the bottom of the staircase was a horror. The humidity and horrid smell hit him first: Mold, mildew and several different types of rot all mixed in together, driving him back a few paces with the strength of it all. The spark of light brightened to fill the entire chamber. Bren could now see in every corner, and he didn't like what he saw.

On the ceiling, bright green slime of some fungus-like kind bubbled and rippled like waves on a lake. Every once in awhile, a large patch of the green mass would fall to the floor. For a few minutes there would be a furious bubbling and hissing where the green blob had landed, and then the mass would turn dark and stop moving. Every wall was coated thick with a carpeting of sticky-looking molds and fungi of some sort.

Out of one wall, two thick brown tentacles suddenly swept out and latched onto pieces of fungi and objects on the floor. As the masses of fungi were swept aside, Bren was stunned to see a Tomtek jar lying there in the middle of the chamber.

The jar lay in a jumble of the bones of some poor fool who must have tried to steal something from the wizard. The fungi had dissolved clothing and scrubbed all the flesh from the bones. But obviously it didn't like the taste of metal, because the man's weapons had been left untouched, although their scabbards, presumably once of leather, were gone. There was no way to tell if the body was a day dead or hundreds of years dead, but there was something almost alarming about the way the sword blade still looked brand-new and razor sharp.

Bren couldn't see any way into the chamber without getting covered in mold, fungi, and slimes, all of which, he thought, were probably able to eat through flesh in seconds.

What could he do?

Maybe, Bren thought, he could change the wizard's mind. *Turn to E8.*

Should he try making a dash for the jar and hope he could press the amulet quickly enough to get out of there? *Turn to E9.*

Or was there something he had overlooked? *Turn to E10.*